PLANET
JOY

D0928763

Also by Jenny Valentine

A Girl Called Joy

Love From Joy

PLANET JOY

JENNY VALENTINE

Illustrations by Claire Lefevre

SIMON & SCHUSTER

First published in Great Britain in 2022 by Simon & Schuster UK Ltd

Text copyright © 2022 Jenny Valentine
Illustrations copyright © 2022 Claire Lefevre

1 3 5 7 9 10 8 6 4 2

Simon & Schuster UK Ltd
1st Floor, 222 Gray's Inn Road
London WC1X 8HB

www.simonandschuster.co.uk
www.simonandschuster.com.au
www.simonandschuster.co.in

Simon & Schuster Australia, Sydney
Simon & Schuster India, New Delhi

A CIP catalogue record for this book
is available from the British Library.

PB ISBN 978-1-4711-9655-3
eBook ISBN 978-1-4711-9656-0
eAudio ISBN 978-1-3985-1713-4

This book is a work of fiction.
Names, characters, places and incidents are either the
product of the author's imagination or are used fictitiously.
Any resemblance to actual people living or dead,
events or locales is entirely coincidental.

Typeset in Stempel Garamond by M Rules
Printed and bound by CPI Group (UK) Ltd, Croydon, CR0 4YY

To all the Bright Sides

1

My name is Joy Applebloom, and I am nearly eleven years old. My family used to be always on the move, in different parts of the world, but then we stopped and came back to the UK, to 48 Plane Tree Gardens, which is where my grandad lives. He is Mum's dad and his name is Thomas E. Blake. Home to him is a tidy house on a street of other tidy houses. The five of us are all packed in tight like sardines in a can, but with a lot more conversation about table manners and a constant queue for the bathroom.

According to my big sister, Claude, our real address is The Square Root of Nowhere. She says if we don't get out of here soon she is going to combust, and the rest of us one hundred per cent believe her. Grandad says he would rather she didn't do it on his hall carpet, because thanks to Dad and a certain dropped cup of coffee, he has just paid to have it professionally cleaned.

When we moved back to live here, there were a lot of quick changes.

Claude and I went to an actual school for the first time ever, instead of doing our lessons on the move.

Mum and Dad started looking for jobs and

flats and doctors and furniture and other long-term things that you can't just put in a suitcase and take with you when it's time to go.

Grandad's house went from so quiet he could hear a pin drop to so noisy he couldn't hear himself think.

We made friends and noise and mess and chaos. And even though we have been here for a little while now, life is still crammed full of upsides and silver linings and surprises.

Claude says, 'You would think that. Even if we were stuck up to our necks in a crocodile-infested swamp in a monsoon.'

My sister thinks I have silver linings drawn on the inside of my eyelids.

Dad says he doesn't want to think about what she has on the inside of hers.

All I know is we are being bombarded with

exciting new things. They are fizzing like just-discovered comets through our sky.

I have a new teacher and a brand-new hobby, and I have started learning a whole new set of languages that I never knew existed.

There is new girl in 6C, who is even newer than me.

Our old teacher Mrs Hunter has a new actual *knee*.

Claude has at least two brand-new political causes. She is very busy getting angry about the state of the world and standing up for things and fighting the oppressor and going on marches. My sister is twenty-four-hours-a-day LIVID, and for once, Mum and Dad say she has every right to be, and that they could not be more proud.

She also has a new boyfriend, and a new

favourite word, which is PRIVACY, and apparently she is not getting any of it. Dad says he doesn't know where she is finding the time for love when she is so busy being absolutely outraged about everything, and Claude sticks her chin out like a fighter and opens her eyes up extra wide, which is her way of saying MIND YOUR OWN BUSINESS.

Grandad has a new interest in gardening because of his new friend, whose name is Miss Hedda Wolfe. Together, they have turned his grey concrete backyard into a flowery paradise, bird-filled and buzzing with bees. It is quite a transformation, and I am not just talking about the garden. Grandad used to be spotless and sort of nailed down and grey, and now his hands are always muddy and his cheeks are mostly pink and his fingers have turned out to be extremely green. It is like the old Grandad got dragged through a hedge backwards, in the best possible way. He used to spend a lot of time sitting very still in a chair and now he is mainly digging or snipping or crouching over seedlings with his bum in the air. He does a lot of whistling. He says Hedda Wolfe has given him *a new lease of life*, and he is grateful because it was me who introduced them.

I look at Grandad's cat, who has a sparkly new collar and extremely high cheekbones and a thousand-yard stare.

I say, 'Well, it was Buster, really.'

Miss Wolfe lives at number 57. Buster used to disappear to have his dinner there and stay the night, and now so does Grandad.

Claude does not want to talk about it.

Dad has just started his new job at the

big community centre at the bottom of Sunningdale, the block of flats on the Meadows Estate where my best friend Benny Hooper lives with his family. It has been *refurbished* which means it is as good as new. Now, the community centre is called My Second Home and it is going to be a drop-in place for the elderly, and a preschool nursery and a library and a café, all in one place, around one courtyard. Dad is the executive chef. This means he is the one in charge.

'Just like at home,' he says, and everyone rolls their eyes. Even Grandad.

When Dad talks about his new job, I can tell how much he likes it. Apparently, the team at My Second Home are performing Community Magic, and Dad says he cannot wait for us to see it. We are all going to the big open day at the end of the month. Grandad is bringing Hedda Wolfe as his plus one, and Benny's whole family is coming, which means Claude's new boyfriend will also be there due to the fact that he is Benny's big brother, Sam.

Claude has a new smile and Mum has bought herself a new dress. Dad says both of these things are delightful and surprising. He calls it *the dawn of a new era*, which makes Claude look like she wants to bury herself head first in the bin.

The new girl in 6C looks like she wants to be buried head first in a bin too. She is definitely not looking like she wants to be in school, that's for sure, and I sympathize because I can still remember how that feels. I think she is very enigmatic and mysterious. So far, Benny says he is finding her about as cheerful as a ghost train and less enthusiastic than a hole in the ground. But something tells me that she is about to come out from behind what is eclipsing her and turn out to be our newest friend. I tell Benny I am almost convinced of it. I am hoping that this feeling isn't what Claude has started calling, 'Life on Planet Joy.' This is my sister's way of saying that I know nothing about the real world and I am way too optimistic about people and life in general. I am crossing my fingers that the new girl doesn't agree with her. Only Claude can make the word *upbeat* sound like it is dripping with poison.

Lastly, I'm almost certain that we won't be staying in Plane Tree Gardens for much longer.

I think I overheard Mum and Dad talking

about it. I'm not supposed to overhear their conversations, so I can't know, but if it's true then we are on the move again, and I'm honestly not sure how I feel about that. The four of us are very good at packing up and saying goodbye to the old things and hello to the new. We have done it all my life, and it has always been pretty brilliant and exciting. But for the first time ever, we have put down some roots, like Grandad's new roses, and we are not nearly the seeds on the breeze that we used to be.

I am on the lookout for more clues, but I am trying not to talk or think or worry about it yet, because I have so many other new things to be busy with. And I am quietly working on remembering the silver linings of our old life on the road. There are hundreds, like having everything you need in just one suitcase, and Dad's fireside songs, and how Mum feels about a sunset, and so many kinds of foods, and the way flying fish keep up with your boat in a clear blue sea.

If we go, Grandad will have his quiet tidy house back. I am wondering if he will miss us and all our chaos at 48 Plane Tree Gardens, or throw a party to celebrate. The new, refurbished version of Grandad means this is actually quite hard to predict.

2

Our new teacher came into our lives out of the blue like a surprise gift, which is much more dramatic and interesting than the kind you've been expecting.

A few Fridays ago, Mrs Hunter thunder-clapped her hands at the front of the class. This was her way of saying she was about to make an important announcement. At the time, I was very busy sticking scrunched-up lumps of black tissue paper on to my model of a bat. I wasn't in 6C at all any more, but in a cave near San Antonio that was overflowing with Mexican free-tailed bats. The air was thick and smelly. The opening looked like a giant's eye in the ground, and the sky around it was a living thing, beating with wings, incredibly loud and incredibly quiet at the same time. When Mrs Hunter told us all to stop what we were doing *immediately* and put our hands in our laps and LISTEN, I had to hurry all the way back from Texas. This is not the kind of extra effort that Mrs Hunter has ever tended to notice or appreciate.

We were supposed to be looking only and exclusively at her. This was way harder than it sounds because we were also trying to look at someone on the other side of the door, waiting to come in. Through the round porthole graph-paper window I could see their hair, which was black and shiny, and a corner of their shirt, which was tablecloth white.

Mrs Hunter cleared her throat and leaned a little bit on her desk for support. She told us she was taking the rest of term off to get a new knee, and she looked straight at me when she said, 'I will allow five minutes for questions.'

New knees are made out of metal and plastic. Doctors move the kneecap out of the way like a sliding door so they can get to the bones behind and then they glue the new parts to the old ones with a kind of cement. Afterwards you have to have painkillers and physiotherapy and a lot of rest, and for a while you will be a bit swollen and have to walk with a stick. You can come back to work when you are good and ready.

Mrs Hunter let in the mystery person waiting outside, and it was as if she had opened the curtains to let in the day. The visitor was a dazzling patch of sunlight. Mrs Hunter was a wet clump of fog. They stood together at the front of the class. When two things are the same but different, like me and Claude, or Dad and the prime minister, Grandad says they are like chalk and cheese. This was more like glitter and brick dust.

'This is Mr Suarez,' Mrs Hunter said. 'He is going to be your teacher while I am away.'

A flurry of excitement broke through the room like a wave. Bailey Parker did a fist pump and I think Mrs Hunter saw it. A sad little shadow scudded across her face. She looked deflated, but Mr Suarez did not.

'Two replacements,' he said. 'One knee and one teacher,' and everyone apart from the wet lump of fog laughed.

Mr Suarez's beaming smile moved over us like a searchlight. His hair was slicked back and shiny under the lights. His trainers had rainbows on them. He seemed electrified with enthusiasm. I already knew I was going to like him.

He said, 'I am super excited to be joining you in 6C. This is my first ever real-life teaching job, so this class will forever be special and I will never forget you.'

Mrs Hunter sighed loudly, like she had just carried a hippopotamus up ten flights of stairs with no help. She was the opposite of electrified. She said, 'I am sure you will all make Mr Suarez feel very welcome,' and then the bell rang for the end of the day.

'Hooray for the weekend!' said Mr Suarez. 'Hip! Hip!' and I couldn't help noticing that Mrs Hunter's face was more like a damp Tuesday in November.

When I started school for the first time, me and Mrs Hunter were not exactly the best of friends. We couldn't agree on anything. My old teacher found me too loud and too opinionated and too fidgety, and I thought she was not friendly enough and very gloomy and much too strict. She didn't believe that I had ever been inside a volcano, or bottle-fed an alpaca, or slept in the foothills of Mount Kilimanjaro, and she definitely did not want to hear about *any* of it. She wanted me to do as I was told and stop talking and be more still and think less thoughts. And I wanted her to relax. She needed me to be a bit less Joy, and I needed her to be a bit less Mrs Hunter.

It took us a while, but in the end, I think we were just starting to understand each other. Mrs Hunter was learning to put up with me, and I was doing my best to cheer her up and keep it zipped. She really made me get better at a lot of difficult things: percentages and fractions, punctuation and neat handwriting. Timetables. And the meaning of words like *intolerable* and *untrammelled* – and *flibbertigibbet*, which has turned out to be one of my all-time favourites.

I'll admit I had high hopes that our new teacher would find me one hundred per cent more interesting and at least three quarters less of a pest. Mr Suarez looked like he might be a lot more curious to know about the way sea-ice sounds almost *exactly* like a snoring giant, or how the buildings of Jaisalmer actually do turn golden at sunset, or the time I saw a black bear, full of honey and fast asleep in a tree. But I was a little wary of finding out. Mrs Hunter did not even pretend to enjoy it when I talked about stuff like that. She did not have the time to listen and she wasn't even one tiny bit inquisitive. I think she is the kind of person that could stand on the top of a mountain and miss the view.

But, like every-single-body in the whole wide world, Mrs Hunter does have her own silver linings, if you just know where to find them. She is keen on historical things, like Grandad, and she knows loads about the outside world. She is kind to caterpillars and she loves chocolate, and she did her best to help me and Benny when we tried to save the enormous ancient oak tree in the playground. When her knee wasn't hurting and we were all very much doing exactly as we were told, she could sometimes almost look like she was starting to enjoy herself in 6C. I knew it wasn't going to be the same at school without her. Mrs Hunter and I might be very different people, but that still didn't mean I would be glad to see her go.

So while everyone else was hurrying out of the classroom and getting stuck in the hallway traffic jam, I took my time packing my pencil case and I put my books in my bag extra slowly. Mrs Hunter says I am a dawdler, which means I take too long to do the things she wants me to be quick at. I could hear the special foot-tap she always does when she feels I am out-staying my welcome in 6C. Mr Suarez had his back to me because he was reading all the workings on the whiteboard. That morning we had been doing long division, which is another thing I dawdle at, mainly because it ties my brain in tight little knots that take about a century to unpick.

'Are you a tiny bit sad to be leaving?' I

asked her. 'Or mostly just excited about your new knee?'

I could tell by her face that she didn't really want to talk about it. 'Oh,' she answered, with zero enthusiasm. 'I'll be back.'

'Well,' I said. 'I will miss you when you're gone.'

Mrs Hunter looked petrified, like I was Medusa and my hair was made of snakes and I had just that minute decided to turn her instantly and irreversibly to stone.

Mr Suarez spun right round on the ball of one foot, with his smile on high beam.

'Well, aren't you kind!' he said. 'What's your name? What a lovely thing to say.'

Mrs Hunter glared at him. She used her hands, palms up, the way Claude does when she's arguing, which is often.

'Mr Suarez. Meet Joy Applebloom.'

And her glare said something much less welcoming than that.

If she contained even just one atom of sadness or excitement about leaving, Mrs Hunter didn't show it. Not a peep. She didn't want any fuss, thank you very much, and she was categorically not interested in a big noisy send-off. Her last week in 6C was just like any other week, apart from a big assembly on Friday, when our head teacher, Miss Stilwell, made a very nice speech. She said the whole school would feel lost without its longest-standing member of staff, and that everyone was already looking forward to welcoming her back.

Later, Bailey Parker said he would not exactly be counting down the days, and Benny pointed out that Mrs Hunter never did stand for very long, but we all clapped anyway, and Miss Stilwell gave her a big bunch of flowers and a card that had been signed by all of the teachers.

Mrs Hunter looked like a beetroot under a raincloud from start to finish. Some people just don't like saying goodbye.

3

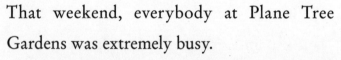

That weekend, everybody at Plane Tree Gardens was extremely busy.

Grandad and Hedda Wolfe were planting trees for bees. I went swimming with Benny at the Lido. Claude was going to a climate strike with her friends from school, and Mum and Dad were meeting Benny's mum and dad for a drink. Our two families have become very good friends. Dad calls us the Applebloopers.

This might be another one of my new favourite words, even if it does make Claude want to dig her nails into the nearest piece of furniture and just *scream*.

Thanks to family mealtimes with my sister, we have been learning about how hard life is for bees because of pesticides and diseases and other things that human beings could stop using and causing and doing.

'Without bees, there wouldn't be much plant life on earth at all,' Claude says. 'Food crops would be down by one third and ninety per cent of flowers would disappear.'

We wouldn't eat avocados or strawberries or almonds or cherries or blueberries or oranges or grapefruit or cucumbers or apples or tomatoes or onions or pumpkins. Claude is a vegan now, and Mum says the silver lining there is that she eats a lot more of the things on that list. And every time we do eat them, Claude makes sure to point out that without bees, their days are numbered. Apparently, there would also be a lot less coffee, which Dad can't do without. This is the sort of topic Claude wants to discuss at the dinner table now – I'm not sure if it's worse or better than when she used to want to discuss nothing at all.

My sister says the bees are very stressed. Dad says he knows how they feel.

'So do something,' Claude says, exasperated, and Grandad says, 'You're right. That's it. I'm planting some trees.'

Hedda Wolfe already has a beehive in her garden. It is wooden and looks like a little Scandinavian hut. She

showed me and Benny the drawers full of waxy and mathematical comb where the honey is stored. The bees were non-stop busy and Miss Wolfe's garden is full of the plants they like to visit. She and Grandad took cuttings and now they have planted them in pots in the garden at number 48. The pots have labels that are lolly sticks in the soil. Hedda has written on them in her spidery handwriting – HAZEL, WILLOW, CRAB APPLE, HAWTHORN, CHERRY AND HORSE CHESTNUT. They are going to have a stall at the community centre open day and they have already donated some of their tiny trees to the garden there. They are also going to give a tree to everyone on the street so that Plane Tree Gardens is a haven for bees. Grandad says that we should call it Bee Tree Gardens from now on. He also says that gardening is rather magical in its own way.

'You stick something in the ground and it just *grows*,' he says, and his eyes are full of wonder.

This is the sort of thing that *he* talks about now at the dinner table, when he used to have even less to say than Claude.

Benny and I have been talking about how we could help at the open day too. We were picking up litter on our way to the pool. It is a bit like looking for treasure, but with much less exciting results. There is way more rubbish on the pavement than there are ancient coins, so it keeps us pretty busy. It might only be three streets and the park, but Claude is always saying that every little helps. It is surprising how many things just get dropped, because there are bins everywhere and there are big recycling ones by the lido. We used four bags:

one for cans, one for paper, one for plastic and one for anything gross. I have told Claude we are doing our bit to recycle and she is very pleased to hear it. She has started wearing a T-shirt that says CLIMATE STRIKER. It is much too big for her and she won't let Mum wash it. This is because it belongs to Sam.

At Sunningdale, Angela saw Claude wearing it and said, 'Oh, I wondered where that went,' and Claude turned the colour of my strawberry smoothie and pretended she was suddenly noticing something out of the window.

When Benny and I got to the Lido, it was crowded

and splashy. The sun was shining and the concrete was hot under our feet and the water was cold and a brilliant turquoise blue. Benny had money for ice cream and I had Claude's old towel with a hood that you can put on like a dress.

I love swimming. Benny says I am as quick as a fish.

I wondered what our chalk-and-cheese teachers were doing with their weekends.

'Mrs Hunter is putting her feet up,' Benny told me. 'And having a good long moan.'

'Do you think she will miss us?' I asked him, and Benny laughed and splashed me.

'Nope,' he said. 'Not for one second. She is glad to see the back of us and have some gloomy quiet.'

'What do you think Mr Suarez is doing?'

I said, but he dived under water like an otter before he came up with an answer, and after that we swam to the side without taking one breath, and by then we had both forgotten the question.

Mum and Dad and Angela and Ed, the grown-up Applebloopers, were going to My Second Home for a look around and then to the pub for lunch.

The community centre on the Meadows Estate was closed for ages before it became My Second Home. In all the times I have visited Benny, I have only ever seen it with the windows boarded up and the outside covered in cobwebs and torn posters and bright scrappy graffiti. There always used to be a big pile of dead leaves and old litter washed up in its dusty doorway, like stuff left behind by the tide.

But the builders had been hammering and drilling away for weeks, and the whole place had been covered in scaffolding and getting a wash and a new coat of paint.

Dad said it was a complete refurbish and mum plonked herself down in a chair and said, 'Oof, I could do with one of those.'

Benny's mum is almost as excited as Dad about My Second Home. As well as the old people's drop-in centre and the nursery and the café, it is also where the new library is going to be after they shut down the old one and turned it into fancy flats. Angela says that the new-look centre actually took years of campaigning and fundraising. She is on something called *the board*, which means she gets to make decisions and is why she knows the whole thing wasn't magicked out of nowhere, like a rabbit from a hat.

'What people need to remember about overnight success,' she says, 'is that it takes a lot longer than one night.'

Ed is very proud of what Angela and the community-centre board have managed to achieve. He says, 'My wife should have been an MP,' and Angela smiles her beautiful smile and says, 'Well, maybe one day your wife will be.'

4

On Mr Suarez's first day as our new teacher,
6C was UNRECOGNIZABLE. Before I even
got to class, I met Benny and Clark Watson
coming the other way down the corridor.
Clark lives in Benny's block too and they
walk to school together most mornings. Those
two have had their ups and downs, but these
days they are mostly on the up, which is a
good thing.

'Where are you two going?' I said, and Benny and Clark stopped walking.

'Oh,' Benny said, scratching his head, and Clark looked behind him, back the way they had come. 'That's weird.'

'Are you lost?'

I meant it as a joke, but then Clark started to explain that 6C wasn't there any more, or at least not where they thought it was.

Benny looked truly baffled. He said, 'How is this even *possible*?' and I pictured the islands that we sailed to in the sea near Athens that were there in the morning, but in the afternoons always disappeared.

'It's this way,' I said.

'You'd think,' Clark said, and the three of us headed back to where our classroom should have been.

'The door is the same,' I said, and Benny said, 'Just wait till you open it.'

And he was right. It wasn't an island that had vanished at high tide, but 6C as we knew it had disappeared off the face of the earth.

Mrs Hunter's dusty all-year-round Kings and Queens of England display was missing and all the pinboards were covered with clean new paper, white and black, with glossy silver edges, like blank canvasses, or switched-off screens. The equipment drawers were at the opposite end of the room, the tables were arranged in brand-new clusters and they weren't even named after colours any more, and there was an enormous shelf that looked just like a pile of books, somehow reaching up to the ceiling on their own. The cobwebs were gone, we could hear music playing and the whole place smelled of flowers and fresh air instead of disinfectant and wee. Everything on the walls was blank and untouched like fresh snow in a Swiss mountaintop village, and it was like a new beginning.

Clark Watson and Benny looked like they'd seen a ghost and found the Gingerbread House all at the same time. Clark's eyebrows shot up like high-flying birds and they took almost the whole day to come down to land.

'Am I dreaming?' Clark said.

Benny was turning on the spot. 'Is this even real?' he said, and I said, 'I think it must be, yes,' and closed my own mouth with my hand.

Clark said, 'Mrs Hunter's kings and queens will be turning in their graves,' and I pictured our old teacher's face when she was cross, pulled drawstring tight, with her eyes like buttons and a very bad smell just underneath her nose. I hoped our new teacher had kept the old royals for her somewhere, and not just screwed them up and thrown them in the bin.

Mr Suarez was standing in the far corner on a ladder, fixing some bright bunting to the ceiling tiles. He leaped down, graceful as a gazelle, and didn't pull a face and complain about his knees even *once*. He was wearing his rainbow trainers and a jumper that was a very precise and brilliant shade of kingfisher blue. His sunglasses were balanced on the top of his head. He looked like he was about to go somewhere nice for lunch. This was not a look Mrs Hunter ever went for or hoped to achieve.

'WELCOME,' he said. 'You're bang on time,' and he handed me, Benny and Clark each a laminated badge with our own faces on one side. 'Write your names on these and pin them to your jumpers, and I will have learned who you all are by tomorrow.'

'That's impressive,' I said, and instead of telling me off for interrupting and not putting my hand up, Mr Suarez *winked* and said, 'Trust me, Joy Applebloom. I am only just getting started.'

Because we were the first to arrive, we watched the rest of our class show up in the same state of surprise and confusion. Everyone got a badge and a friendly welcome. It was more like coming to a birthday party than a Monday at school.

Most people believe that in the southern hemisphere, which is the bottom half of Earth, the water goes down the plughole in the opposite direction to the top half, which is the northern hemisphere. I have tested it and it isn't true. Not in a sink anyway, although it does work on bigger things like ocean currents and hurricanes.

6C was a bigger thing.

It felt like an ocean that had moved from one hemisphere to the other. Everything was back to front and upside down and topsy-turvy. Benny kept going the wrong way for the scissors, and more than one person seemed caught out by where the door was. I watched people doubling back on themselves or stopping suddenly in the middle of the carpet before switching direction, and it put a warm flame in the very middle of my stomach. Hedda Wolfe says 'a change is as good as a rest', but I think it's something more exhilarating than that. A change is as good as a rickshaw ride on a three-lane roundabout in Hyderabad, or a plunge off a boat deck into the deep wild, dark-at-the-bottom sea. My face ached from so much smiling.

If Mrs Hunter had been there, she would have needed smelling salts, or a lie down, I guarantee.

'Look at these plain old walls!' Mr Suarez said, lifting his arms out wide and turning in a circle, while we all just looked on, awe-struck. 'We'd better do something about them, don't you think?'

Instead of the dusty old kings and queens, we were going to draw our own self-portraits, which Mr Suarez called *selfies*, with paints or chalks or pastels or charcoal or collage, 'Or all five if you want to, and don't worry about the mess.'

While we were drawing them, we were also going to do mental maths, which involved a lot of thinking with our voices and calling out the answers. It was noise and colour and laughter and making and learning, all in a jumble, which was not the kind of Monday morning we were used to, and might just be my school version of perfection.

Mr Suarez said, 'What's four hundred and fourteen divided by two, plus eight, times four, minus twelve?'

All you could hear was the whole class scribbling and cutting and sticking and discussing and counting until somebody called out the right answer, which was, 'Eight hundred and forty-eight!' and Mr Suarez threw his fists in the air and the class cheered. The maths got harder and harder, the room got quieter but noisier and our selfies got brighter and better and it was the most extraordinary morning in 6C *ever*. When the bell rang for first break, nobody wanted to leave the classroom. Not one person leaped to their feet and barrelled to the door like in the old days. Even Bailey Parker looked disappointed that it was time to go out and play.

Out in the playground, you could see all the little groups that make up our class going off like fireworks, telling everyone else about Mr Suarez's new-look 6C. Becky Charity and her girl gang said making selfies was the best possible lesson ever, and it was a relief to finally have a teacher with some style. Naseem Choudhury and Bailey Parker and the other football-kickers said Mr Suarez looked pretty fast on his feet and was definitely a decent transfer. Farah Charles and the cool kids leaned against the wall under the arches and admitted he was *all right*. Me and Benny and Clark walked around the edges of the asphalt digging for buried treasure in the dirt with the toes of our shoes, all the time knowing that the real-life treasure was, at that very moment, in the staffroom, making new friends and dazzling people with his smile.

'Well,' Benny said, taking off his glasses and polishing them on his shirt. They were smudged with pastel and covered in fingerprints. 'That was exciting.'

Clark said, 'I'm out of breath like I've been running around, not just doing *maths*.'

'What's going to happen *next*?' I said, and all of us agreed that it was going to be *something*.

5

Maybe it was because Mr Suarez was so excitable and distracting that it took me and Benny so long to notice that our teacher was not the only new person in 6C. It was as if, right after break, there was suddenly a new girl. I still have no idea when she actually appeared. The exact same moment I saw her for the first time, Benny nudged me with his elbow and said, 'Who's that?'

The new girl was sitting across from us on the table under the window. One minute she wasn't there at all, the next she was kind of quietly taking up the corner like someone who had just stealth-landed and then slipped off their invisible cloak. If I believed in magic that's exactly what I would have said had happened. But I don't, or not the storybook kind, so the next best explanation must have been that she was keeping herself to herself, and feeling shy.

Mr Suarez had renamed our tables after famous composers. Me and Benny were on the Bach table and Clark Watson was on Vivaldi. The new girl was on Mozart. Benny knows a lot about classical music. He said that Mozart wrote his first piano concerto when he was eleven, and that the Mozart table must be for people with the biggest ideas. He also said that our group was called Bach because we are so good at working together as one, and that this is what Bach's music is known for, and we should take it as an excellent compliment. He told Clark Watson that Vivaldi is extremely popular, which was exactly what Clark Watson needed to hear. If there was a table for people who know how to say just the right thing, it would be called a Benny Hooper.

The new girl's hair was black and her fringe was long, like a curtain. Her self-portrait was heavy and thick with charcoal. Me and Benny both smiled at her across the classroom and she glowered back. A glower is something halfway between a glare and a frown and Claude is very good at them, and so was the new girl. When her eyes met mine I thought about dank caves and underground spaces and flickering candles and cold nights. I thought about bats and owls and panthers and shadows and witches. And it was only when she blinked slowly and looked away that all the lights came back on in the classroom and I was back in the real world again with all its daylight and colour.

Benny couldn't read the name on her badge from where we were sitting because his eyesight wouldn't stretch that far, but I could. And it didn't surprise me.

The new girl was called Phoebe Dark.

For our first piece of homework, Mr Suarez made up a sort of quiz for us all to answer about who we were and the things we liked and what we spent our time doing when we weren't spending it at school. He said he wanted to get to know us before he made some decisions about how to run the classroom. He said he was *information gathering* and that we all needed to know what made each other tick.

He said, 'Information is the *key* to understanding. And UNDERSTANDING is the key to everything else.'

Benny leaned over and said out of the side of his mouth, 'I have never seen a grown-up this enthusiastic.'

And it was true. 6C was more like a TV show than a classroom.

'Tell us some things we don't know,' Mr Suarez was saying. 'Surprise us. Surprise yourself! Be unexpected. Be hungry to LEARN.'

He had already answered his own quiz and pinned it on the wall by the door so that we could read it. The whole of 6C clustered around it, like ants on sugar, gathering information, even if it was only fun facts about our new teacher, and not the causes of World War One, or what the secret chemical symbol for salt is, or the mysteries of nine to the power of three.

Mr Suarez had very flowy handwriting like a ribbon in the breeze.

Name: Gabriel Suarez (like the angel).

Nickname: Gabo. Gabolito. You can call me Mr S.

Favourite things: Coffee, sunshine, polvorosas cookies (my grandmother's recipe), musical theatre, kick-boxing, scuba diving, open-top cars, running marathons, learning new languages, swimming, mountain walks and wildflowers, black-and-white movies, long train journeys and all of you in 6C!

Best school subjects: *History. But in 6C we will call it OURstory. And dance!*

I took my quiz home and talked to all the people in my family and asked them for tips to help me answer it correctly and not miss anything out.

'Talking,' said Claude. 'You love *talking*,' and Grandad said, 'You are very good at remembering to feed the cat.'

Mum said I liked new places and snorkelling and Dad reminded me of how much I loved chameleons and then Claude said, 'You actually *all* love talking, don't you?' and went upstairs for some privacy in our room.

I took my time and tried my best to be neat, apart from a couple of splotches, and in the end I went all out and decorated my form with a rising sun and a crowd of daffodils with smiling faces. There wasn't enough room on the form to fit all of the things I love, so I just chose twenty-one.

LIKES + DISLIKES

Name: Joy Applebloom

Nickname: I don't have one. But Mrs Hunter had lots of names for me, so maybe you know some already.

Favourite things: Talking, reading, running, travelling, humans, treasure, Benny Hooper, sunsets, swimming, snorkelling, handstands, chameleons, funfairs, vegetable samosas, my family, trees, bees, silver linings, tuk-tuks, letters and the moon.

Best school subjects: Art and geography, but I am willing to have others.

6

People say that my name suits me because I am cheerful and optimistic and I have a habit of finding the good in things and enjoying them. I think that Phoebe Dark is more than living up to hers.

She lurks in corners and hides in the shadows. Claude often talks about what look she is going for, like, 'Tree-climber, but in heels,' or 'Eco-warrior, but not *crochet*,' and

I think that the look Phoebe Dark is going for is a black space in a Technicolour cartoon. She wears only black clothes, seven days of the week. Even her socks are black. She paints her fingernails black with felt tips when she has finished writing up science experiments or drawing diagrams of average rainfall in Bavaria, or working out what x equals when y equals thirty-two.

On the weekend she wears black eyeliner the same way Claude used to, like a drawing of an eye on plain paper, except that the paper in question is her own face. I know this because I have seen her skulking through town. I think she was with her mum and her little brothers. The boys had matching pirate hats and little swords. They looked like twins. And her mum was laughing into her phone while Phoebe

Dark stuck to shady places like the sunlight might hurt her.

Benny said she looks *nocturnal*. He said she has the sort of style that might like a bed that is shaped like a coffin, if she goes to bed at all.

'She's not a vampire,' I told him. 'She's an ordinary human, like us.'

'Well,' Benny said, 'I wish she would cheer up and start enjoying it, whatever she is.'

We were handing in our forms to Mr Suarez first thing while he waited by the door. Mine was pretty crumpled. I can get carried away when I'm colouring, and this used to drive Mrs Hunter to *distraction*. I tried to smooth it out against my leg before I gave it to him and I said, 'Sorry if it's a bit of a mess.'

Our old teacher would have made her mouth

into a tight straight line, like a ruler made of disapproval, but Mr Suarez was smiling.

'Oh no, that's fine,' he said. 'Let's face it. Who doesn't want to liven up a boring old form?'

Some of the favourite things on Benny's form were about music, because that's his thing. He is studying for grade six violin, and in the whole world of grades there are only eight. That's how brilliant he is. He put *Joy Applebloom* on his list too, though, in between *the weekends* and *my mum's pancakes,* and I said, 'Well, that's lucky, seeing as I put your name on mine.'

Bailey said he liked being a striker and didn't like being in goal.

Clark wrote that his favourite person was his big brother, Jet.

Becky Charity's said she was really into

photography since her uncle gave her his old camera.

Phoebe Dark's form was scrunched up in a ball and scrawled all over with black ink. It was as dark and murky as her self-portrait. She handed it to Mr Suarez like it was a top-secret document that was about to self-destruct.

Benny leaned into me with his hand over his mouth and whispered, 'Maybe she's a double agent for Mrs Hunter. Perhaps the stealth new girl is a *spy*.'

7

I have been very happy living at 48 Plane Tree Gardens, with all of us piled in together. I do not think it is the square root of nowhere at all. I think it is the centre of our family's very own universe. I definitely do not want to leave. Not yet. Not when we are finally all settled. But if the universe is constantly expanding, which is apparently a true thing, then I suppose it is also true that ours is going to need to expand soon as well. Maybe that's why Mum and Dad have been talking about moving. The other day, I saw them with a load of packing boxes. Even though I was dying to ask what was going on, I decided not to. Claude thinks I should try to be less nosy, and, anyway, I didn't want to know the answer.

I am guessing I will find out soon enough.

In the meantime, it is a bit crowded. Mum and Dad have to sleep on the sofa in Grandad's living room, and I have to share a bedroom with Claude, who likes to lie down a lot, and on her own, thank you very much, and not anywhere near me. This means I have had to get good at finding other places to be. It used to be quite easy to curl up with a book in an armchair or squirrel away with my schoolwork to the kitchen table. But now Grandad and

Hedda have a new lease of life together and are covering everything that doesn't move in flowerpots and a coat of bright paint, it is getting harder than ever.

Benny's mum, Angela, has always said I can be at their flat whenever I like, and I do love it at 114 Sunningdale, where Benny and Sam and Angela and Ed Hooper live, eleven floors up with a view of everything. But lately this also happens to be another place where Claude is busy trying to get her privacy, and so even that isn't as simple and straightforward as it was before. Because of Claude's new boyfriend turning out to be Benny's big brother, Sam, these days she is at Benny's house as much as I am.

I put Claude and Sam in the same hiding place behind the wheelie bins at Benny's treasure hunt birthday party, so they could jump out and surprise him. They are the second pair I have brought together, after Grandad and Miss Wolfe, and I think this makes me a qualified matchmaker, but Claude says, 'Don't lump me in with those two. They have a combined age of one hundred and forty-six. It gives me the Ick.'

'Thomas and Hedda up a tree,' Dad sings, to give her even more of one. 'K-I-S-S . . .' and then Grandad walks in and Dad stops and the air is thick suddenly. And warm. You could butter it like toast and use Dad's cheeks for jam.

Sam Hooper is about eight million times nicer than Claude's last boyfriend, whose name was Riddle. Benny's big brother smiles and talks in whole sentences and, according to Dad, both of these things are signs of significant progress.

Sam Hooper cares about the same things that Claude does and he loves listening to her stories the same way Benny likes hearing about mine. He knows a lot about fossil fuels and civil rights and vegans. He is funny and nice to look at, and he plays the cello and the violin. Claude cheers up a lot when she is near him, and I am very happy for her and, come to think of it, also happy for everyone else. I'm so glad she likes the Hoopers as much as I do, and gets to see for herself how much fun it is to be around them.

When Benny and I want to watch cartoons on the TV, Claude and Sam move over on the sofa so we can all fit. This doesn't sound exactly groundbreaking unless you have lived at 48 Plane Tree Gardens, where Claude usually leaves a room if more than one person walks into it, and spends most of the time she is awake complaining about having to share the shower with three generations, or a double bed with me.

At 114 Sunningdale, I am learning to share my best friend's house with my sister and I think she is learning to share her boyfriend's house with me.

One of the best new things about it is when we walk home together. I think Claude has noticed the way Sam always asks Benny how school was, and has questions about Mr Suarez and trigonometry and our geography homework like he has a) remembered their last conversation and b) is actually interested. Benny's brother talks a lot more about his day than my sister ever used to talk about hers. Where I would normally settle for 'FINE' as a description, Benny gets details about football teams and music teachers and the cafeteria and something to do with a broken locker.

So these days, when we walk back from Sunningdale, Claude talks. A LOT. It is a refreshing and an eye-opening change.

She tells me about her school climate-strike group, and about the *curriculum*, which is a long word for the stuff we learn, and very one-sided apparently, and 'policed', and 'an actual scandal'.

'You and I, Joy,' she says, 'have learned all sorts of things by just *being*. But at school, the actual GOVERNMENT gets to decide what we all know.'

When she says it her eyes are as big as saucers and she is wobbling her head. She looks like the beautiful giant string puppet we saw of a

Syrian girl, Little Amal, on the last part of her 8,000 km journey as a refugee. When I point this out she says, 'You see? We *walked* with Amal, we were *there*. At school you just get to read about it in a book, if you're lucky, and THEY get to decide what books you have and what you read, if you read it at all.'

'Who are "THEY"?' I ask her, and string-puppet Claude lifts her hands and her head wobbles some more.

'I don't know,' she says, and her voice drops to a whisper, 'but they are *everywhere*.'

This new Claude is a lot more informative than the old one, who had forgotten that she knew things and mainly started to worry about what her bum looked like in jeans instead. When I am not overhearing Mum and Dad talk about packing, I have overheard them saying that Sam is a very good influence on her, and I think it is true. At Sunningdale, Claude offers to lay the table, or do the washing-up, or sort out the recycling, before she is even asked. She sits on chairs instead of lying across them and she walks without stomping and she smiles with her lovely white teeth showing for more than one thousandth of a second, and she speaks so you can hear her, instead of pulling the neck of her jumper up over her whole mouth or muttering into her sleeve.

I make a mental note to tell Mum and Dad about the Sunningdale version of my sister. Dad says that it's *gratifying* to know your children have good manners somewhere, even if that somewhere is nowhere near you.

8

Everyone in my family is getting a bit tired of me talking about my new teacher. Claude has been telling me to give it a rest and for once nobody is arguing with her. But I don't think I could actually stop, even if I wanted to, because he is fascinating and dazzling, and always coming up with something brilliant and new.

Take school clubs, for example.

Not that long ago, before Mr Suarez and

Phoebe Dark arrived, there were zero school clubs, except for a breakfast one, which Benny says was rubbish because everyone was still half asleep. He only went because his mum was running it for a while, and because he could have the mini-variety cereal boxes that he's never allowed at home. According to Benny, even variety boxes lose their appeal when there is less than half a bucket of Lego and four sheets of coloured paper between fourteen of you and it's not even eight o'clock.

Then, pretty soon after he became our teacher, one Friday at the end of assembly, Mr Suarez made an announcement about after-school clubs. He stood up and glided over to the microphone like he was on skates and the whole school held their breath to listen.

'Guess what!' he said, while all the other

teachers sat with their eyes on their own shoes. 'It's CLUB TIME.'

After we had finished cheering, he said the school needed helpers from Year Six. Nearly everyone in 6C put their hands up and he picked Benny and me. We had to go to the head teacher's office for a chat, because Miss Stilwell is fond of those. Mr Suarez was there too. It was all his idea to have new clubs because he had them at the place where he learned to be a teacher and they were *phenomenal*. Miss Stilwell suggested four clubs to begin with: chess club and cookery club and nature-watch club and gym club.

We suggested archaeology club, because one of our favourite things to do is look for buried treasure.

Mr Suarez suggested drama club.

Benny asked if we could put all the suggestions to a vote and see what was most popular and have room for some other ideas too, and Miss Stilwell kept her mouth closed and her hands in her lap, which is her way of saying NO.

The rules for school clubs are like all the other rules at school: complicated and strict. We are not allowed to do things on our own, in case something goes wrong and somebody gets hurt. There has to be one wide-awake teacher or sensible grown-up for every more-or-less handful of us. When I mentioned this at home, Claude said that she had *had it up to here* with not being trusted. She looked right at Mum while she was saying it. This has got something to do with her not being allowed in her bedroom with Sam Hooper with the door closed. I said that according to Miss Stilwell, the rules were less about trust, and more about keeping us safe, and Mum looked right back at Claude then, and raised her eyebrows, and said, 'Exactly,' and my sister gave us one of her special silent, withering scowls.

Claude told me it would be impossible to convince grown-ups and teachers to spend extra time doing things that sounded like more work. She said, 'Teachers aren't babysitters, you know.' But, really, me and Benny and Mr Suarez just figured out what people like doing, and then asked if they have one hour, once a week to do some more of it. I think it turned out to be quite easy. For example, Mr Hannerty, whose class is 4H, and who wears socks with different superheroes on from Monday to Friday, told us that he loved teaching under-elevens chess more than life itself. And Miss Baxter, the PE teacher, said there was nowhere she would rather be on a Wednesday afternoon from four to five than helping us get better at handstands and bridges and cartwheels. When I told her that, Claude insisted they were both lying. She called me an *actual dummy*. But Mr Hannerty and Miss Baxter are both running clubs now, so I'd say that is speaking for itself.

I did ask Mum and Dad if they would like to be in charge of any after-school clubs because Dad is a brilliant cook who knows a lot about maths and judo and, amongst other things, Mum is good at first aid and riding bikes and juggling and talking about books. I thought they would jump at the chance to help, and they could make friends with other parents while they were doing it. I had it all planned out. But when I suggested it, they looked at me like they had forgotten I was in the room, or even speaking, and that was kind of that. At the moment, they seem to be the run-off-their-feet version of busy. They say things like, 'I am meeting myself coming back,' and, 'There just aren't enough hours in the day.'

I have taken this as a *No*.

Luckily, Benny's mum's answer to the same question was a *Yes*, and so now she is in charge of bakery club. This happens on Wednesdays in the school kitchen, which is a place we aren't normally allowed to be in, and feels a bit like going backstage at a show. So far, we have made cheese straws, brown bread rolls, cinnamon swirls, banana muffins and flapjacks.

CHEESE
STRAWS

We each bring 50p every week and that buys the ingredients for the week after. Angela says it is a very efficient system, and that I have a definite flair for a good bake. She says if we keep this up, we could bake some goodies for the open day at the community centre.

Nature-watch club is doing something for the community centre too. Miss Stilwell has given us our very own patch of school garden, about the size of twenty-four maths books. It is on the outside wall of 6C and has a perfect mixture of sun and shade. There are eight of us in nature-watch club. We have planted special shrubs to attract butterflies for our insect count. We have planted sunflower seeds in little pots so we can sell them at the open day and help to fundraise. We've made a bee hotel out of cut-up bamboo stalks inside a wooden frame. And a boy in Year Four called Robin knows how to build a hedgehog house out of a shoebox and some leaves and straw. We have been learning about the different kinds of creatures who share our school, and there are way, *way* more of them than we thought. Lastly, we are planning a pond so that we can see the life cycle of a frog for ourselves, in the real world, and not just read about it in a book. It will be about the size of a sink, and lined with black plastic, and it involves a lot of digging. Miss Stilwell is in charge

of that one, but she says on the weeks she is busy we might have some special guests. I have already told her that Miss Wolfe and Grandad could be two of them. They have already promised to give us some trees for bees. Dad says there is a swampy corner at My Second Home and that maybe nature-watch club could have a My Second Pond there too.

Everyone agrees that school clubs are brilliant, and also that they are all thanks to Mr Suarez.

'Wait until you meet him,' I tell my family, while Claude rolls her eyes and Grandad does something on his kitchen windowsill with more sunflower seeds and Mum yawns into her laptop's face.

Dad says, 'I already feel like I've known him all my life,' and I say, 'SAME!' until I realize he is teasing.

Mr Suarez's smile is like strip lighting – the kind that ticks and blinks on and can illuminate a speck of dust. I wonder if he switches it off at the end of the day or just falls asleep with it still shining. He is the sort of person Grandad would call flamboyant, like a peacock, or a dancer at a carnival. The old Grandad would have meant it disapprovingly, but the new Grandad would say it as a compliment. Mum says Hedda Wolfe is a proper miracle worker, and I think Mr Suarez might be one of those too.

According to our new teacher, there are all kinds of different ways of learning something, and we each have our own special favourites. These days in 6C we are allowed to read out loud and make up songs and walk around and even bounce a ball or catch a beanbag while we are trying to remember things. We can use pictures or words or songs or even jump up and down if it makes the facts go in and not come straight back out again.

'Whatever suits you,' he says, like a showman, receiving applause. 'Whatever works.'

He says that if you are going to find out about democracy, you should ask for the vote and stage an election. If you want to learn about Italy, it is best to use Italian words and eat Italian foods and watch Italian TV shows and read Italian books and wear Italian clothes and talk about Italian history. This is what he calls Full Immersion Learning.

'Get your F.I.L.!' he says. 'Your FILL!' and I can tell by his face that he has just-that-minute thought of it.

When I say that at home, even Grandad, who

is normally so accommodating, mutters, 'I've just about had my fill of this fellow now too.'

Mrs Hunter used to stick to a dog-eared, out-of-date textbook and had us copy down what was written on the board. Sometimes it was hard to remind the blood to keep circulating in your body. Sometimes my feet went to sleep and I worried that the rest of me would quickly follow. There is no danger of snoozing with Mr Suarez around. He is the opposite of Mrs Hunter in every way. He stands up straight and has very white teeth and he is *always* smiling – even, or especially, when the classroom is full of noise and mess. At the exact times when she would have her hands over her ears and a face like thunder, he throws his arms out wide and says, 'Look at you all, just getting on with your *learning*.'

Sometimes when I talk without putting my

hand up, or take too long finishing a piece of work or make too much noise reading in the quiet corner, I expect Mr Suarez to give me a dark, stormy look or say my name in a razor-sharp voice or sit slumped in a chair like a just landed parachute because there is no hope of fixing me. But he never does. He says, 'Where has Joy got to this time?' and, 'That book must be *very* funny,' and, 'You must PROMISE to tell me about that at break time.'

Mr Suarez leaps around like the floor is lava. When he reads he uses different voices for different characters and does all the actions and he asks loads of questions about what we are all doing so that sometimes it almost feels like we are teaching him.

6C used to feel like a waiting room or an airless cabin; now it is something between a beehive and a party. It is an excellent feeling.

I think he is most definitely my favourite kind of teacher.

But in the back of my mind I have still been thinking about Mrs Hunter and what she is doing with her time. I have been crossing my fingers that she is happy in her own way and not missing us. I have been wondering if she is coming back next term or not. And I have been hoping that she won't mind too much when she finds out that, without her, school is suddenly the brilliant thing that I'd always hoped it would be.

9

When I told everyone at home about Phoebe Dark, Claude said she sounded *cool*. And she is. Very. Like a lake in winter, or an early morning in Svalbard, or an invisible and very slippery patch of black ice. I have enjoyed myself in all of these places, so the frosty new girl wasn't worrying me. Not yet. Not completely, anyway.

Mr Suarez did not seem to be Phoebe Dark's

kind of teacher. Every time he spoke to her, she looked like she wanted a hole to open in the floor and swallow her up. Now I have spent a bit more time around her, I would say it was a black hole. The kind that live in space and can swallow gravity and change the speed of time and are actually an absence of light.

But, slowly, something has started to change. Like a thing that's thousands of light years away finally coming into view.

I think it started with the class presentations.

Mr Suarez asked us to turn our personal quizzes into a sort of little speech to the whole class. We had to stand at the front and tell 6C our top favourite facts about ourselves. If we wanted to do anything else, like a demonstration, or what Mr Suarez called *a little flourish*, we were more than welcome.

Bailey Parker demonstrated that he could eat more than fourteen Jaffa cakes in under a minute. It was quite impressive and also maybe put me off eating them for life.

Benny flourished with his violin skills, and afterwards Mr Suarez wiped the tears from his eyes with a bright red handkerchief. He said, 'You must play with my great-aunt Estelita. She was a concert pianist in Venezuela. The two of you together would be *divine*.'

Naseem Choudhury did keepie-uppies with his football on the reading carpet and everybody clapped along to encourage him and he got to 105, which Mr Suarez said was *spectacular*. It would have been even more if Mrs Bird from 5B hadn't put her head round the door and asked us to please keep the noise down, which put Naseem off his stride and stopped him from breaking his own personal record, which is still 142.

Clark Watson did a magic trick that was actually so brilliant the whole class asked him to do it twice. I still don't know how he made the card vanish and then show up in his own back pocket. Clark says his lips are sealed and he will take it to his grave because it is the magician's sacred duty to never tell.

I did a sort of slide show of the best places I have ever done a handstand. Claude has taken a photo of me doing handstands everywhere we have ever been, so I have loads of them in a special folder on Mum's laptop. I chose my six favourite photos, which are: the Grand Canyon, Monteverde Cloud Forest in Costa Rica, Varanasi on the banks of the Ganges, upstairs at the Statue of Liberty, inside a

sleeping volcano in Iceland and in the middle
of the Colosseum in Rome.

Mr Suarez thought I was showing my skill at computer graphics until he realized I had actually been to all of those places for real.

He said, 'Well, I am *speechless*,' and Bailey Parker frowned and called out, 'But you just said it, so technically you're not.'

This kind of answering back used to add up to earning Bailey Parker a trip to Miss Stilwell's office, but Mr Suarez just laughed and said, 'Clever, Mr Parker, and also true.'

Then Benny carried on telling him that I had been travelling about all over the world since I was born. He said, 'Joy can speak three and a half languages. She has been in more countries than I've had hot dinners.'

Mr Suarez was about a hundred times more impressed by this than Mrs Hunter had ever been.

'And how does 6C compare?' he asked me, and I clicked on my last picture, which Benny had taken of me doing a handstand in front of the whiteboard one break time in a thunderstorm when Mrs Hunter had gone to investigate a roof leak and wasn't looking. It's not my best one because we were in a hurry just in case she came back and blew her top.

'Nice shoes,' Mr Suarez said, noticing in the photo that I had written on the soles of my own trainers, the words 'smile' and 'please'.

Mr Suarez's best and most fascinating fact about himself was that he used to be a professional actor and dancer and that he had appeared on stage in London and Broadway, in more than one extremely famous musical. He sang us a song about gravity and everybody gave him a standing ovation, which means we stood up and clapped instead of staying in our chairs. Clark Watson stuck two fingers in his mouth and whistled. It was the sort of morning that would have given Mrs Hunter chronic earache.

When it was Phoebe Dark's turn to tell us her favourite thing, she looked uncomfortable and odd standing at the front of the class. Like a blob of ink on a clean pillowcase, or a patch of silence in a forest of birdsong. She stared out from behind her curtain fringe and her eyes darted from side to side, like the tadpoles in our new pond. It was the first time she had seemed like she was about to speak. Everyone watched and waited. I expected her to sound shy and nervous, but when she finally used it, her voice was strong and powerful and determined.

'My interesting fact hasn't happened yet,' she said.

'Okay,' said Mr Suarez, uncrossing and crossing his legs like he wasn't in any rush. I couldn't help thinking that Mrs Hunter would have told her to hurry up and get on with it. 'Tell us anyway,' Mr Suarez said, as relaxed and comforting as a beanbag on a Sunday afternoon. 'And take your time.'

Phoebe Dark drew herself up to her full height. With her black clothes and her black shoes and her black hair she looked like an exclamation mark. She took a big deep breath.

'I am going to be the first woman to land on the moon.'

10

Claude has had Careers Week at school. She had to do a quiz too, but hers told her to be a hairdresser when she really wants to study engineering, and she was fuming like a fire-breathing dragon about it. Grandad said she had a bee in her bonnet and Claude said, 'I don't even own a bonnet. This is exactly the kind of language that keeps women in their place, and I will not be tolerating it from anyone, least of all YOU.'

Grandad was about to say something else, but Hedda Wolfe jumped to her feet, surprisingly nimble, and clapped her hands and said, 'Yes, Claude! YES! Our fight goes on!' so Grandad bit his tongue and kept his thoughts to himself.

This is what I would call a wise decision.

A very long time ago, when she was younger, Hedda Wolfe was a leading light in the fight for equal rights in Sweden. She and Claude have started huddling in corners talking about the patriarchy and every day Hedda brings Claude more books to read about it. She says that the Swedish are light years ahead of us when it comes to *the struggle*, and they still aren't there yet. 'Not even close.'

I am learning a lot about the history of how unfair men can be. And even Phoebe Dark is helping. I have already decided that she would get on very well with Claude and Miss Wolfe. Last week she wrote an essay about how full of boys the space exploration industry is. Mr Suarez thought it was so good and so interesting that he read it out loud to the whole class. I can see why Phoebe Dark is on the Mozart table.

In her essay, she wrote that only fifteen per cent of astronauts are women. Of the 500 people that have flown in space, only sixty-five haven't been men. She said that the gap was closing, but not fast enough.

'There are ten people in space right now,' Mr Suarez read, and he looked up at the low classroom ceiling for a long time, like he needed to think about it.

'In every walk of life,' the essay concluded,

'women are catching up with men. Even in outer space. So look out!'

Claude is writing an essay too. She is calling it her Feminist Manifesto and it is full of mathematical proof of unfairness, just like Phoebe Dark's essay was.

Dad says it is very good to see his first-born child with her nose in a book, and Claude says, 'Actually, I'm reading three.'

She has started asking a lot of questions about things that happened in history, like the suffragettes and World War Two, and women generally refusing to go back inside and have babies and make the dinner and do what they were told. She has loads of things to say about gender rights and equal pay and glass ceilings and the old boys' network.

Dad says, 'I think I preferred it when you

were mainly grunting and staring at your phone,' and Claude neutralizes him with an icy grin and says, 'I bet you did.'

Mum said I should invite Phoebe Dark over. She didn't know why it was taking me so long.

'You've started talking about your new friend almost as much as you do about your teacher, and we haven't even met her.'

Dad said, 'Is that even possible? Surely there aren't enough hours in the day for more than Mr Suarez?' and I say, 'What new friend?'

'The new girl,' Mum said. 'The one on the Mozart table. The one with the fringe.'

'Oh,' I said. 'That new friend. Really?'

'You were new once too, remember, not that long ago,' she told me, like I had somehow forgotten.

I hadn't forgotten. Usually I would be the first person to suggest something like that, but Phoebe Dark wasn't actually my friend yet. And she didn't seem interested in making friends or being invited anywhere. Even less interested if the invitation was coming from me. I had a very strong suspicion she was finding me annoying, the way Mrs Hunter used to, or Claude still does when she is in one of her shadowy moods. More than once, Claude has told me that my sunny disposition is *beyond irritating*. I think Phoebe Dark would completely and vigorously agree.

The truth is, I had already tried.

After her speech about being an astronaut, and her essay about unfairness in space, I was ninety-nine per cent sure that Phoebe

Dark and I would have lots to talk about. For a start, I knew she would enjoy a game of Good-For-You.

This isn't a family invention, but it's something we have always done. According to Mum and Dad, girls aren't good at saying out loud what they're good at. They say that most boys will tell anyone who's listening that they're life-changingly *brilliant* at stuff, even when they're not. ('Trust me,' Dad says, holding his hands up. 'Guilty as charged.')

But girls need encouraging.

That's why they started it, when we were very little, and that's basically the game. Claude and I have already played it at Sunningdale with the Hoopers and they loved it. Especially Angela, who did a lot of WHOOPING and cheering. It's simple to play and you don't need any equipment. You just take turns saying what you're good at, and everyone else has to shout 'GOOD FOR YOU'.

Some people think saying what you're good at is arrogant and pure showing off, but Mum and Dad always just called it common sense. Everybody is good at something, that's what they say. Plus, it makes people feel better about themselves on bad days, and it's actually much more fun than it sounds.

For example:

Mum is good at bandages and driving big trucks round small corners and juggling and staying calm in a crisis.

Dad is good at telling jokes and sailing and riding a bike up steep hills without once getting off.

Apart from being extremely good at being

moody and asleep, Claude is also good at running, origami, plaiting hair, drawing, learning languages, and crosswords. And right now she is really good at caring about the planet and feminism and the climate crisis and Sam Hooper.

Sam Hooper is good at the cello and making smoothies and being a big brother and making Claude smile.

Angela is good at painting and dancing and laughing and telling stories and making you feel like the sun is out even when it's raining. She *loves* a game of Good-For-You. She put her arms round me and Claude after the first time we played, and said, 'I am going to teach *all* my girlfriends this so they can teach *all* their daughters,' and then she waggled her finger at Ed and the boys and said, 'Watch out, these women are coming for YOU.'

Ed is good at roller skating and singing and knowing about jazz and making doughnuts from scratch.

I can't think of one single thing that Benny Hooper *isn't* good at.

I am good at imagining, making friends, swimming, fractions, finding silver linings and making tea. I am also very good at Good-For-You. The trick is to say things without hesitating, like you're one hundred per cent convinced you have a talent for it, even if you're secretly not. And the more you say it, the more you start to remember that it's true.

I already knew that Phoebe Dark would have a long list of things to say she was good at. At break time, she was sitting on her own under the big oak tree. The rest of the playground was like Mumbai central train station, loud and colourful and frantically dashing this way and that.

I did not need a reminder from Mum or anyone else about how it felt to be new here, and a bit different, so I ducked under the oak's low branches, the same way Benny once did for me.

'Hi, Phoebe,' I said.

Phoebe Dark had her eyes closed.

'It's Joy.'

She opened them, grey as thunderclouds, and looked at me with something halfway between patience and fury. 'I know who you are,' she said. 'Where's the other one?'

'The other one?'

'The boy. The one you're always with.'

'Oh!' I said. 'Benny? He's playing football.'

'Right.'

Phoebe Dark blinked very slowly, the way Grandad's cat, Buster, does when he is just about tolerating you and doesn't want you to forget it.

'It's nice under here, isn't it?' I said. 'Nice and peaceful.'

'Very.'

She didn't look peaceful; she looked annoyed.

'What are you up to?' I said.

Phoebe Dark's sigh was long and slow and exasperated, a bit like one of Mrs Hunter's. 'I am trying to think.'

'What about?'

She smoothed her hair down and put her hands in her lap. They looked like two sleeping doves. She didn't answer my question.

'Do you need something?' she said.

'No. I just thought you could do with a friend,' I said, and Phoebe Dark's eyes got even darker, like two thunderclouds filling up with rain. Her dove hands flew at me the way Claude's do when I am a fly she wants to swat and a buzzing she wants to silence.

'Honestly, what I could do with,' Phoebe said, 'is some silence.'

'Really?' I said, but Phoebe Dark had finished talking to me. She closed her eyes again and sat as still as the trunk of the tree. Not even her eyelids flickered. And the annoying buzzy fly that was me backed away.

Later, at 114 Sunningdale, Benny made ice-cream floats and Sam and Claude were tickling each other on the sofa. At its sharpest, Claude's laugh was a knife-edge.

'Am I annoying?' I asked Benny over the noise of the blender and Claude's squealing. He looked at me and burst out laughing. I noticed that his glasses were being held together at the bridge of his nose with a plaster. He noticed me noticing.

'It's all I could find,' he said. 'Your sister just sat on them.'

Claude scream-laughed again. Benny let go of the blender and put his hands over his ears. 'And by the way,' he said, talking to me, but looking at her and Sam, 'you are the most UN-annoying person I know.'

'Well, I don't think Phoebe Dark agrees,' I told him.

'Really?'

'Or Claude, who is my own *sister*. Or Mrs Hunter.'

Benny pushed his sat-on glasses back up his nose. 'Mrs Hunter isn't our teacher right now. And she was a fun-sponge,' he said. 'Claude is a mood board and sometimes she doesn't like *anyone*. And Phoebe Dark just isn't a silver-linings, glass-half-full kind of person.'

'You think?'

'She's what my dad calls a *cool customer*,' he said. 'Doesn't mean she doesn't like you.'

'I don't know,' I said, and Benny smiled. 'Well, not knowing something has never exactly bothered you before.'

'That's true.'

He handed me my ice-cream float. It looked spectacular. Like an iceberg on a lemonade sea.

'You're not a quitter, Joy,' he said.

'I'm really not.'

'So.' Benny shrugged like it was that simple. 'Don't give up.'

11

Every single class in the school was starting a new project about Planet Earth at the same time. We were all going to make them ready in time for parents' evening. They would be parts of one giant display through the school building.

Mr Suarez said, 'We are going to WOW your parents and carers with what we all KNOW.' He also said this meant that 6C had to put our skates on and choose our project, *double quick*.

We were each allowed to put one thing into the big ideas shoebox. Mr Suarez had covered it in silver paper and cut a slot in the top and put a big label on it that said SUBMISSIONS. He was going to pick his top two at lunchtime and then we would get to have a vote.

'So put your reasons together,' he said. 'Because if your idea gets picked and you want to win the final vote, you will have to tell us WHY.'

Mr Suarez was wearing his badge that said: GOOD LISTENER. I looked at Benny and he looked at me and we were both smiling. Benny's eyebrows would have been way over the top of his glasses if he had been wearing them.

'Uh oh,' I said. 'Did you forget your glasses?'

'Nope.' Benny grinned. His eyes were even more sparkly and bright than usual.

Without his glasses, Benny usually has to hold a thing right by his nose if he wants to read it. But his book wasn't by his nose. It was down on the table, same as everybody else's.

'How can you see what you are doing?' I said.

Benny's grin was off the charts, up there with Mr Suarez's high beam. 'Contact lenses,' he said, putting his face close to mine. 'I finally got contact lenses. LOOK.'

Benny's eyes are large and round and warm and brown. His eyelashes are surprisingly long. Claude says she would kill for eyelashes like Benny's. 'And Sam's,' I tell her, and Claude blushes and pretends that she is searching for something very vital and urgent at the bottom of her bag.

I looked carefully at Benny's eyes and I could just make out a very faint line around his pupils, like the line of the newest sliver of a moon before it gets dark. He said this was the edge of his new lens.

Benny had been waiting to get contact lenses for ages. Angela said they are quite fiddly and you need to be able to poke yourself in the eye without actually poking yourself in the eye, and also be very good at taking care of them and not forgetting they are a) in or b) out. Benny had proved that he was capable and now he has his reward.

'That's *amazing*,' I whispered.

'Claude helped,' he said.

'How?'

'By sitting on them, remember?' Benny said. 'That's a silver lining if ever I saw one.'

'Definitely,' I said. I couldn't quite stop trying to work out what was different about his face.

He looked the same as ever and also instantly different. I have never really seen him without his glasses, apart from when we go swimming at the lido, where he looks streamlined and underwater, same as everybody else does. Right now, Benny without his glasses was looking to me like Benny who had forgotten to finish getting dressed.

I said, 'The change is very hard to put my finger on.'

'Same,' said Benny, and he moved to push them back up like they were slipping, even though they weren't there any more.

According to Benny Hooper, new things sometimes take some getting used to before they feel as comfortable and as easy as the old ones. His face might have altered, but I am saying he is still just as wise.

'But I love them,' he said, and went back to enjoying doing his reading from a pleasingly long distance.

Mrs Hunter never liked us talking in class, unless we had permission to talk to her, or had been specifically instructed to talk to each other, so when Mr Suarez came over to me and Benny at our table, we thought we were going to get a telling-off. I could feel us both getting ready. Benny sat up even straighter than normal and I tried to appear very hard-working and serious and quiet.

'You two look happy,' Mr Suarez said, and he didn't sound annoyed about it at all.

'We *are* happy,' Benny told him, and I said, 'Benny's got new contact lenses.'

'OH!' said Mr Suarez, and he put one hand on my shoulder and one on Benny's, and

BEAMED. 'I wear those too. They are a game changer, let me tell you. Oh, what a happy day.'

When Mrs Hunter paid a visit to your table, it was like a passing raincloud. Mr Suarez was more of a sweet-smelling breeze. It was a big change. We were still very much getting used to it.

My idea for our class project was the oceans. I have swum and sailed and snorkelled in quite a few, and in my mind's eye I thought of us all learning different things about them – all the life above and below the water. I could already picture our spectacular display, with jellyfish and hermit crabs and giant whales, and vast trenches that are blacker than night, and ocean liners and deep-sea explorers.

Benny chose deserts, and Clark went for

the Ancient Romans because he knows a lot about them already and it seemed easy. Bailey Parker said he picked climate change, but at break time, someone from 5B said that was their project already. Becky Charity wanted us to do migration, and Naseem said, 'Birds or people?' and Becky Charity said, 'Both?'

After lunch, Mr Suarez showed us the emptied shoebox and read out all the different ideas before he announced the two he had chosen. There was an empty biscuit wrapper and an elastic band in the box too, and he picked them out and dropped them from a great height into the bin.

'Those ideas were nearly winners,' he said, and everyone laughed.

Mr Suarez is extremely tall and willowy. At certain angles he reminds me of a giraffe.

I was regretting not putting *watering hole at the savannah* as my suggestion, when he held up a piece of paper with blue waves drawn on the back.

'This,' he said, 'is one of our final two. Whose is it? The oceans.'

I put my hand up.

'And this,' he said, holding out a black piece of paper with silver writing on it, 'is the other one. Whose is this one?'

A ripple went through the classroom, a quick holding of breath, because Phoebe Dark had put up her hand. She doesn't do that very often. Basically never.

'Mine,' she said, and her eyes darted about like trapped mice under her curtain of hair.

Mr Suarez's fluorescent smile was even brighter than normal.

'By George,' he said, even though there is no one called George in 6C. 'That's an interesting one. Not quite what I expected. But, on reflection, I think we can include it.' And then he read hers out loud too, holding it in his other hand. 'The planets.'

There was a hush and then a sudden round of applause, and underneath her fringe, I am pretty sure Phoebe Dark's eyes were twinkling like distant stars.

Phoebe Dark and I had to take it in turns to explain our ideas. I went first because Mr Suarez told me to. I pretended I was playing a game of Good-For-You so that I could sound confident and like I knew what I was talking about.

'The oceans are full of life and other mysteries,' I said. 'There are five oceans on our planet – Atlantic, Pacific, Southern, Indian and Arctic. They are all connected somehow, so actually there is really only one ocean, and it covers more than seventy per cent of the Earth's surface and holds ninety-seven per cent of the whole planet's water. It is so large that only five per cent of it has ever been explored. The Pacific is the biggest ocean. It is one hundred and sixty-eight million square kilometres, which is about three hundred Europes, plus a little bit more. The Mariana Trench is the deepest place on Earth. If you put Mount Everest at the bottom, it wouldn't stick out above the water at all. The words "ocean" and "sea" are often used to mean the same thing, but seas are really just the parts of the ocean where water meets dry land. There are about one million species of animals living in the ocean. Earth is almost all water. Because of this, the more we learn about our oceans and seas, the more we can begin to fully understand our beautiful watery planet.'

By the time I had finished, I was a Mrs Hunter scale of beetroot red, but everybody clapped and Benny said, 'Well done,' and I got some pats on the back from people behind me so overall I think it went fine.

Mr Suarez said it was, 'Excellent.'

Then it was Phoebe Dark's turn. 'Make your case, Phoebe,' Mr Suarez said. 'Tell us why *all* of the planets belong in our school project about Planet Earth.'

She stood up and faced the class. There was a definite gleam in her eyes. She was practically lighting up in her shadowy corner. I had forgotten how commanding and determined her voice was. She knew when to talk and also when to pause so that we could think about what she was saying and let it sink in. For somebody so quiet, she is a very brilliant communicator.

'Currently,' she said, and everyone stopped moving a muscle and paid attention, 'we can see very deep into space. The Hubble Space Telescope has recorded some of the furthest galaxies, thirteen point two billion light years away. This means it took thirteen point two billion years for the light created by those galaxies to reach us. The universe seems infinite. It might be another thousand years before we can begin exploring these distant planets, but because we can see them, we know that they *exist*. We have explored about five per cent of the bit we know is there, but there is much more that we haven't even discovered yet. That's like realizing there are five million oceans. When we learn about our solar system and all the other galaxies, we learn where our planet fits in something much, MUCH bigger than we can even begin to imagine. We learn to know our place.'

Mr Suarez said Phoebe Dark's presentation was *excellent*. I voted for her idea because it was fascinating and better than mine. I wanted to tell her that, but I didn't want her to give me one of her glowering looks, or think that I was being annoying, so I just clapped extra hard when she won and said, 'Well done, Phoebe.'

I'm not sure she heard

me, because she was surrounded by people asking her questions. Mr Suarez gave her the whiteboard marker so she could write down all the different possible subjects of our topic. At the top of the board she wrote in big bold black letters:

THE KNOWN UNIVERSE.

Bailey Parker nudged me in the ribs with a big grin and said out loud, 'Maybe we'll find somewhere even Joy Applebloom has never been.'

12

I told Claude about Phoebe Dark and how much I was sure she didn't like me and how hard it was to try to get through to her. Claude has a very different way of looking at things, and sometimes this can be frustrating, but sometimes it can also be very helpful. I was hoping for some tips.

'She thinks I am bothersome and irritating,' I said. 'I have tried being friendly and inviting her to do things. She just hangs about all by herself. If Benny put her in one of his cartoons she would have her own black cloud following her everywhere.'

'Maybe she likes it,' Claude said.

'Likes what?'

'Hanging about by herself and being moody and mysterious.'

'Who likes that?'

Claude sighed. She stopped walking.

She said, 'You think I want to be on my own at home because I don't like any of you. But it's not that simple. I want to be on my own sometimes because I *like* being on my own. It's not anyone's fault. You aren't doing anything wrong.'

'I'm not?'

'No. You're not. Well. Most of the time.'

'Thanks, Claude!' I said, and I gave her a hug.

'Ugh. Don't ruin it,' she said, but she did hug me back.

We walked for a bit and then I asked her, 'So are you telling me to leave Phoebe Dark alone, then?'

'Maybe. Until you've learned her language.'

'Her language? She has to speak English in the classroom, same as everybody else.'

Claude rolled her eyes and I thought she was about to say something short-tempered and dismissive, but what she actually said was extremely enlightening and very useful indeed. Once I understood it.

'Not *that* kind of language.'

'Well, what kind, then?'

'You've done this a million times, Joy.'

'Have I?' I said. 'What do you mean? Done what?'

'What words did we learn when we wanted to make friends with those girls in Karachi?'

'Some scraps of Urdu?'

'And what did you learn to do to impress Joseph in Zanzibar?'

'I learned to kick the ball with the side of my foot.'

'What does Grandad do for Hedda when she has finished tidying up his flowerbeds?'

'He makes her a cup of tea and gets her a cushion to put her feet on.'

'What does Benny really appreciate when you remember to save it for him?'

'The puzzles section of Grandad's newspaper.'

'What does Dad make Mum for breakfast on her day off?'

'Black coffee and two boiled eggs with toast and marmalade on the side.'

'CORRECT,' said Claude. 'You've got this, Joy. That's the *language* I'm talking about. It's not always words. And once you've got it, you can't forget it. It's just like riding a bike.'

I didn't say anything because I was thinking about all the friends Claude and I have made and all the different ways people do it and all the ways me and my sister get along even when we don't. And at the same time I remembered what Mr Suarez had told us about the different ways there are to learn.

We are all so different.

Sam likes his music LOUD and I have noticed that Angela and Ed are always dancing. Clark was mean to Benny for a while, but only because life at home was hard work and he was feeling angry and left out. Inviting him to Benny's birthday party and sticking up for him when he was down was how we started to put things right again. I have made friends without using any words at all, just by knowing what someone else likes and enjoys. For example, the time Claude and I gave our skipping rope to two sisters in Naples, or the way me and Benny saw treasure everywhere, from the word go, before we even knew that we would be the best friends ever.

'Everyone has their own language and their own way of doing things,' Claude said. 'Pay attention and learn the *difference*. Something will make this Phoebe Dark *tick*. And the same thing doesn't work for everyone. Remember, when I tell you, that we don't all live on Planet Joy. What works for you doesn't necessarily work for everyone. You are going to need a different approach.'

'But when I am anywhere near Phoebe Dark I feel tongue-tied and silly and like I'm not making any sense.'

This is a rare example of a new thing that I don't like. I *never* don't know what to say, but it happens when I want to say stuff to Phoebe Dark.

Claude said, 'Sometimes it's about knowing *what* to say, and at others it's about knowing not to say anything at all.'

'What does *that* mean?'

Claude started counting out questions on her fingers.

'What cheers me up when I am grumpy?'

'Chocolate biscuits and an arm tickle.'

'What makes you feel better when you're sick?'

'Watermelon.' Every single time.

'In a boring waiting room, would you rather have music or a book?'

'A book,' I say. 'And you would pick music.'

'See?' Claude says. 'You know me well enough to know. You just don't know yet what Phoebe Dark would pick.'

And because she was proving she could read my mind, Claude added, 'What's the thing that Phoebe Dark likes doing?'

'She is obsessed with outer space,' I said. 'She's going to be an astronaut. She says she wants to be the first woman on the moon.'

'GOOD,' said Claude. 'I like her already.'

'And *she* would like *you*,' I said. 'She just doesn't like *me*.'

Claude gave me a very serious look.

'Joy Applebloom, I have never in the history of EVER met someone who doesn't like you.

Even when I can't stand you I like you. You are kind and funny and generous and caring and smart and cheerful and positive and *fun*. Stop thinking about if she likes you and start working on how you can speak *her* language and make yourself understood. Move to Planet Phoebe. Everyone has their own language and you and me are pretty good at learning new ones. So learn Phoebe Dark's.'

Information is the key to understanding. That's what Mr Suarez said when he gave us our quiz on his first day as our new teacher. Thanks to Claude, I was determined to be on the hunt for the key to Phoebe Dark, because of the other thing he said, which was, *Understanding is the key to everything else.*

13

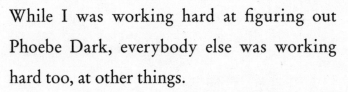

While I was working hard at figuring out Phoebe Dark, everybody else was working hard too, at other things.

Mum is a nurse at the big hospital that looks like a spaceship crash-landed on the edge of town. It is enormous and very shiny and full of tiny windows. Her shifts are non-stop busy, start to finish, and she says she probably isn't getting quite enough sunlight, but apart from that, it's not bad.

Benny's mum Angela works at the hospital as well, on reception, so now she has three jobs, as well as being on the community-centre board and doing bakery club with us on a Wednesday. Mum says she doesn't know how Angela does it, because she is pretty worn out with just the one.

I asked Dad about what was happening at his new job at My Second Home. He had been talking a lot to other people about his vision for the elderly drop-in centre, and the nursery school and the space in between, and how the old and the young would be able to mingle freely in the café and the library and how good it was for everyone. He told me how much we were all going to benefit from something like this in our community. When he told Miss Stilwell about it in the playground, she said, 'If my mother was alive now, she would be in there like a shot. Front of the queue. You are working a miracle.'

When I asked, he just said, 'You will have to see it to believe it.' He said that trying to put it into words couldn't really do it justice.

'I'll tell you one thing, though,' he said. 'That place is *alchemy*.'

I have looked alchemy up in the dictionary and it is something to do with making gold out of pretty much nothing, which sounds even better than a silver lining to me. So I was looking forward to seeing that for myself.

When I told Claude, she rolled her eyes into the back of her head and said, 'Name one thing you don't look forward to,' and for the first time since Mr Suarez arrived at 6C I was officially speechless, and Claude said, 'There. I rest my case.'

Meanwhile, speaking of old people, Grandad's walk is practically a skip. He has started wearing a straw hat. At a jaunty angle. And whistling. He gets up *with the lark*, which means extremely early, and all week he has been clearing out the garden shed. It started because he thought he might have some things to donate to the community centre. And then at some point he also decided to give the shed 'a full makeover'.

Mum says this is not a phrase she ever thought she'd hear her own dad say.

When we got back from Sunningdale, the shed makeover was in full swing. Miss Wolfe had come over to help. She was wearing dungarees and she had tied her hair in a little bun and filled it with clips and combs. Grandad picked a flower and put it behind her ear.

Claude said, 'Tell me this isn't happening,' but I couldn't, because it very much was.

Grandad said he was going to paint the old brown wood the colour of a blackbird's egg, a kind of greenish-blue like the sea on a good day on top of very white sand. Miss Wolfe was already busy planting a big pot with dark pink geraniums to go by the door.

Together they were trying to empty the shed completely and lay everything out on his neat emerald patch of lawn. Grandad said he was only going to put back what he actually needed and was definitely going to use again. Everything else, apparently, had to go. To My Second Home or to anyone's home, just not this one.

'I have been holding on to things for years,' he said. 'And for the life of me I can't remember why.'

The shed was like the magic porridge pot in the fairy tale. It didn't seem to matter how much they kept taking out of it, there was always more.

'It is the gift that keeps on giving,' I said, and Mum said, 'I'm not sure if Grandad is seeing it like that.'

The lawn was completely covered in stuff. You could hardly see a blade of grass. There were cobwebs stuck to everything, and those fluffy lumps of spiders' eggs. There was a legion of hollowed out old woodlice everywhere, like emptied shells.

Miss Wolfe was making three piles: one for recycling, one for charity shops and one for keeps.

'We are a hive of industry,' Grandad said, and Miss Wolfe buzzed and used her hands for little wings and said, 'Yes, we are two busy bees.'

There wasn't an awful lot that looked good enough for donating to a community centre. A museum maybe, or a science experiment about what happens when you leave things in a shed for decades at a time. There were some mean-looking shoes with spikes in the bottom that Miss Wolfe said would be good for aerating the grass, a tennis racquet made out of wood and bent as a banana, roller skates that Mum had when she was the same age as Claude and grass seed that had been sitting under a drip and grown itself into a whole meadow inside the bag. There was fertilizer and old bird feeders, and a moth-eaten badminton net. There were three pairs of wellies that had been nibbled like Swiss cheese by the mice. There were stacks of yellowing newspapers and a beer-making kit that Mum said Dad gave to Grandad about seven birthdays ago. There were some desiccated hyacinth bulbs that Miss Wolfe called *brave* and popped into some soil immediately, *just in case.* There were two bright folding chairs and a box of old hats and some binoculars for birdwatching. And, right there, lying on the lawn with everything else, was the thing I had been searching for, the possible key to understanding everything I needed to know.

A TELESCOPE.

It looked as if it must have been very futuristic about fifty years ago. Underneath all the grime and leaf dust and bits of bird poo and spider fluff, it was black and white and made of smooth shiny plastic. I knew for a fact that we could find it a much better home than in the long-lost back of Grandad's shed.

'Could you donate this?' I said.

'Heavens!' said Grandad. 'Do I own a telescope?'

'I guess so.'

'Yes, Joy,' Grandad said. 'Somebody should definitely put that to good use.'

Hedda Wolfe wiped at the telescope with an old tea towel. The white plastic gleamed underneath the thick coating of forgotten dust.

'Is it working?' she said, and I told her I didn't know.

'We need an expert,' Grandad said, and I already knew just where we could find one of those.

'THIS IS PHOEBE DARK'S LANGUAGE,' I said, very loudly, to Claude, who was in the corner on a deck chair with her nose in one of Hedda Wolfe's books.

She looked up and smiled. 'Jackpot,' she said.

'One person's old is another person's new,' Hedda said, going back to the shed to help Grandad with a set of squirrel-chewed suitcases.

I couldn't wait to tell Phoebe Dark what Grandad's 'old' might be. This was my chance to ask for her help, and finally start speaking her language.

Suddenly tomorrow morning at school felt an impossibly long wait away.

14

Phoebe Dark's way of talking is peppered with star-spangled references to outer space. She talks about the planets and the Pleiades and Orion, as well as the Andromeda and Triangulum galaxies. She knows the difference between meteors and comets, a supercluster and a supernova. She has two cats called Sirius and Cassiopeia. She draws diagrams on the whiteboard and on the back of her exercise books while she is talking, and when she has finished my brain has turned to scrambled eggs and everything I thought I'd ever known is less than one grain of salt on top of it. She doesn't speak in riddles; she speaks in miracles. Her sentences make me feel like an atom in a hurricane because that is exactly what I am.

She wants to have lots of letters after her name. I have no doubt that she will.

In the classroom, once she has started talking about outer space, Phoebe Dark doesn't seem to want to stop.

But out in the playground she was still keeping herself very much to herself.

Benny said, 'I'm not surprised. She must need a rest. I need one too. My head is spinning.'

'Like the planet on its axis,' I suggested.

'Exactly.'

Since the class project started, everything we thought and saw and heard and even dreamed about somehow seemed to have something to do with outer space. Becky Charity and her friends were orbiting around the football pitch like planets round the sun, or moons around the planets. Naseem Choudhury was wearing a hula-hoop, like one of Saturn's rings. All the little people-clusters were like tiny galaxies and the footballs and tennis balls were zipping around like satellites and shooting stars in the sky.

I had already explained Claude's whole language theory to Benny. I'd told him that I had high hopes that Grandad's telescope would be the key to understanding Phoebe Dark's.

Benny was a bit baffled. 'Just pretend that Phoebe is related to Claude,' I said. 'But with astronomy thrown in instead of politics. It makes it much easier to understand her.'

He pulled his thinking face, which is easier to see now he is glasses-free, and doesn't involve the nose-scrunch that was just to keep them from slipping.

Benny likes Claude, even when she is being spiky and crabby like a cactus-wearing lobster.

'Good tip,' he said. 'I feel better about Phoebe Dark already.'

I still hadn't told Phoebe Dark about the telescope. I was summoning up the courage to go over and invite her to Plane Tree Gardens so that she could have a look at it. I was worrying that my key wouldn't fit the lock and that she was going to look furious again and just say NO.

Benny offered to come with me.

'Really?'

'Yep. I'm guessing that two space probes are better than one.'

We wandered over to the big oak tree. Phoebe was sitting underneath it, as usual. She was reading a book called *Calculating the Cosmos*.

Benny pulled a face that meant, *I am smart, but I don't even understand that title.*

I pulled one that meant, *I know exactly how you feel.*

We ducked underneath the branches together, into the quiet shade.

'Hi, Phoebe,' I said, and I tried to sound casual and breezy, and to ignore how reluctantly she tore herself away from the page.

'Hi,' she said, and Benny waved, just with the tips of his fingers. Phoebe Dark frowned.

'I've got something for you,' I told her.

'Oh? What's that?'

'It's at my grandad's house,' I said. 'I found it in his shed. He was having a clear out and giving it a makeover.'

'That's nice,' Phoebe said. 'What is it?'

'Oh!' I said. 'Sorry. It's a telescope.'

Phoebe put her book in her lap. This was a start. I kept talking.

'He forgot he even owned it and it's just lying there. I've cleaned it up a bit and it looks quite fancy.'

She brushed her hair out of her eyes, which were sparkling and bottomless and *smart*. 'Interesting,' she said.

'I thought so. Do you want to come and look at it? We would like your expert opinion. And you would be welcome to use it.'

'*Use* it?'

'Yes. I mean, if you don't have a telescope at home already.'

'I don't,' she said. 'I have twin brothers that break things while shouting.'

'Oh,' I said. 'That sounds noisy.'

'It is,' Phoebe said. 'I actually come to school for some peace and quiet.'

Benny started backing away.

'Okay, then,' I said. 'We'll leave you in peace.'

Phoebe Dark looked at me through her fringe. 'I'll come,' she said. 'Where does your grandad live?'

I had written our address down for her already on a Post-it, just in case. I handed it over and she put it between the pages of *Calculating the Cosmos*, like a bookmark.

'We'll be there all day on Sunday,' I said.

'Benny will be there too because his whole family is coming for lunch.'

Phoebe's eyes flickered over Benny and then back to her book. She was not finding the Sunday lunch detail very riveting. 'Thank you,' she said, and then she went back to her reading and we were dismissed.

'Wow,' Benny said when we were out from under the tree again and back in the daylight. 'She's actually quite scary.'

'Yes,' I said. 'Talking to her is like getting to the very edge of our own solar system.'

'*One step for JOY,*' Benny boomed. '*One giant leap for JOY-kind.*'

15

The Hoopers see so much of me and Claude, at breakfast, lunch and dinner, that Mum and Dad invited them round for Sunday lunch, just to say thank you. Dad was pulling out all the stops with the menu. All of the Applebloopers were looking forward to spending the day together.

On Sunday, the house felt very overcrowded, even before any extra guests arrived, and the sun was shining, so Grandad suggested we take the kitchen table outside. He was keen to enjoy his colourful new garden and show off his just-finished and very tidy blackbird's-egg shed. Mum and Dad carried the table out through the back door, and Claude and I brought the chairs.

Even Claude was happy about the plan, because Sam was going to be there.

She might be furious with men in general, but she is definitely not furious with Sam Hooper, partly because of his eyelashes, and also because apparently he is a feminist too. She says that Dad and Grandad could learn a thing or two from him, if they made the effort.

'Duly noted,' Grandad says, and Dad says, 'Right you are,' and I wonder if either of them are actually listening or taking this as seriously as they should.

'You can't teach an old dog new tricks,' Mum says, but Hedda Wolfe shakes her head and says, 'That's where you're wrong. It is never too late to learn something new.'

Hedda Wolfe came for lunch too, of course, and we had salad as well as roast potatoes, and Angela brought a fruit tart and home-made ice cream, and the whole garden was a riot of colour and music and laughter. Ed said 48 Plane Tree Gardens looked like the Chelsea Flower Show, and he was particularly impressed with Miss Wolfe's potted geraniums.

Claude sat next to Sam at lunch and showed him how excellent she is at napkin origami, and she also told him what the word for boyfriend was in ten different languages. Sam Hooper looked so proud to know her.

'How great is it that Claude got the highest

mark in the whole school for her essay?' he said, and Mum said, 'What essay?' and I said, 'Her Feminist Manifesto,' and Hedda Wolfe clapped her hands together and said, 'Oh, darling! Did you win the prize?'

'What prize?' said Dad.

Claude was looking shy and a little bit embarrassed and also more than a little proud of herself for doing something brilliant and secret at the same time.

'Why don't we know about this?' said Mum.

'Oh, we've all had a crash course in feminism over at Sunningdale,' Ed said. 'In fact, we got you something,' and then he and Sam and Benny all took off their jumpers and they were wearing black T-shirts with FEMINIST written on them in big pink letters. There was one for Dad and one for Grandad too, and when they put theirs on it was Claude's turn to cry, even though she was happy. She wasn't the only one. Hedda Wolfe's eyes were streaming and her voice was all watery with pride.

'That's my girl,' she said, and Claude hugged her and said, 'THANK YOU. I couldn't have done it without you.'

It was the best day at Plane Tree Gardens ever. After the fruit tart, when the sun was quite low over the fences and the sky was turning the same pink as Miss Wolfe's favourite rose, there was a knock at the door. We all heard it because it was loud and quite decisive and just on the edge of being impatient and cross.

'Who's in trouble?' said Dad, and I noticed straight away that Angela and Mum both started counting, to make sure we were all there.

Benny and I looked at each other. We knew exactly who it was. I had just forgotten she was coming because of all the other excitements.

Phoebe Dark was here to look at Grandad's telescope and give us her expert opinion.

'It's for us,' I said, and Benny and I jumped up and went to the door together. There was the smell of roast potatoes and strawberries in the air. The grown-ups had drunk more than one glass of wine, and Ed had already turned the music up twice. Angela's laugh sounded like little bells rolling down a hill.

Phoebe Dark stood on the doorstep like the deepest patch of night.

'Hello,' Benny and I said at the same time, and then, because Phoebe wasn't saying anything, I added, 'Come in.'

Phoebe Dark followed us into the bright

garden like a black cloud at the seaside or a shadow over the sun.

'Everyone, this is Phoebe,' Benny said, and Phoebe nodded instead of speaking.

The Applebloopers waved back.

'Oooh, hello, Phoebe Dark,' said Claude, 'I've heard a lot about you,' and Sam said, 'What's that on *your* T-shirt?' and Phoebe looked down at her own chest.

'A black hole.' Phoebe cleared her throat and looked around the garden without moving anything apart from her eyes.

'She's come to see the telescope,' I said, and Grandad got up out of his chair and opened the door to his shed. He was wearing one of Miss Wolfe's headscarves round his neck like a cravat and he had her pink gardening gloves sticking out of his pocket. He was as different to the old Grandad as May is to December.

'Your Sunday is very colourful,' Phoebe Dark said, and for the first time I heard something almost like approval in the tone of her voice.

And when Grandad came back out of the blackbird's egg and handed her the telescope, Phoebe Dark's face lit up like the moon in the sky.

'It's a 1976 Skybolt original,' she said, quite breathless, holding it like a newborn baby or a just-rescued turtle in the crook of her arms. She placed it carefully on the garden wall and took a cloth out of her pocket, the sort Benny was supposed to use for cleaning his glasses before he got his game-changing new contact lenses. Phoebe Dark was checking the lens on the Skybolt. She looked at Grandad and then at me with a newfound affection.

'It's in really good condition,' she said. 'Thank you for taking care of it. This is a real find.'

Grandad looked a bit nonplussed, seeing as the care he had taken was to forget that it was even in the shed. But Phoebe's delight was contagious. She was checking over the 1976 Skybolt like it was the most precious thing in the world.

She knew exactly what make and model it was, and she knew exactly how to use it.

'Would you like a demonstration?' she said, suddenly not quiet and shy and gloomy at all.

'Yes, please!' I said.

'Of course we do!' said Benny, and everyone else agreed.

It was getting dark. Phoebe started setting the telescope up on the lawn to demonstrate. 'It won't be long now.'

And in Grandad's flourishing garden, with the sun sunk and the sky turning a sort of blackish purple, she taught us all about what we could see. When the sky was finally dark enough, we were the class and Phoebe was the teacher. It was hands down and without a doubt one of the best lessons I have ever had. And that includes all of Mr Suarez's.

'You are a very good teacher,' Hedda Wolfe said, as if she was reading my mind.

'Thanks,' Phoebe said. 'I'm trying to educate my little brothers. You are much better listeners than them.'

Through the telescope we took it in turns to look at Mars and Jupiter and Saturn and the North Star and Arcturus and the Big Dipper. Phoebe knew the answers to all of our questions. Every single one. She could read the night sky like Benny can read music and I can read writing.

She is not a black hole in the corner of things at all. She is an astonishingly powerful fission of fascinating space facts.

She even showed us where she is going to work when she is a grown-up, which is on the International Space Station. It was moving past, 320 kilometres above us in a very straight line, like a motorway or a landing strip in outer space.

She said, 'Three hundred and twenty kilometres is nothing in space. It's like living next door, or on the same head of the pin.'

Mum asked Phoebe if she needed to let

anyone know where she was. She got out her phone and sent a message to her parents. She even showed Mum their message back.

'It's fine,' she said. 'They're busy putting the twins to bed. It takes ages. I gave them your address. They know I am visiting friends from school.'

Behind her, Benny did a winner's jog, and I couldn't switch the smile, Mr Suarez style, off my own face.

Phoebe was looking quite hungrily at all the leftover food, and Angela made her a plate.

Claude said, 'I like your eyeliner,' and Sam said, 'Are those trainers originals?' and I noticed that Phoebe Dark's own glowing smile was like the moon shining out from behind the clouds.

At parents' evening, our classroom was like

the inside of a theatre. It was so dark that Dad trod on Mum's toe and I almost tripped over my own chair. It was Mrs Hunter's idea of a health-and-safety nightmare. There was some quite dramatic music playing, which Benny said was called 'The Planets' by Gustav Holst. Mr Suarez flicked a switch and the ceiling of the classroom turned into the night sky, with stars moving across it, and planets turning in their orbits round an enormous golden sun. The whole of 6C and their parents did a collective gasp. It was like we were standing on the space station. Or at a real-life planetarium.

You could see our new teacher's smile, even in the dark.

Benny said, 'It is like a supercluster.'

Mr Suarez had sweets on his desk for people to take, and cushions on the hard-backed chairs and a jam jar full of pink roses. On the way home, Mum said, 'I see what you mean now, Joy. Your new teacher is amazing. I think I might be half in love with him already.'

And Dad said, 'Yes. Well, move up a bit because so am I.'

16

On the big open day, My Second Home was as polished and shiny as Grandad's windows or Mr Suarez's teeth. There were big colourful flags outside and one of those funny giant people that look like they are dancing because they are being constantly pumped full of air. It was sunny and bright in the courtyard. Sunningdale loomed above us like a mirrored giant, catching the light.

Phoebe Dark came with us. She had agreed to do another one of her brilliant Skybolt demonstrations at the community centre. Dad and Grandad and Angela had all asked her, at different times, so she must have known that they meant it. We knew she would be amazing, and we told her that too, but I think she was still a bit nervous. She stood behind me and Benny like our shadow.

'Are you all right?' Benny asked her.

Phoebe was wearing black sunglasses. She nodded. Benny said, 'We will take that as a yes.'

The whole place was really busy and full of Benny's neighbours. Clark Watson was there with his mum and his brother, Jet. Angela and Ed were helping out on the cold-drinks counter, and Sam and Claude were there too, although they mostly seemed to be holding hands. Dad was wearing his chef's uniform and being the executive of a big barbecue in the middle of the courtyard. The air around him was quivering with heat. All the doors to the courtyard were open and there were café tables outside near where the nursery children were playing with their sandpit and their water table. Some of them were riding their tricycles round and round the courtyard and some of them were playing hopscotch and some were just drawing on the ground with big chalks.

Dad smiled all day and hugged people and flipped burgers. He made a very short speech and said that food can make new memories and also be a way to remember some old ones.

'Take Estelita,' he said. 'She loves my *huevos rancheros* because she says they take her back to her grandmother's kitchen and when she eats them she is eight years old again. Estelita is one of my favourite guests.' And he used his oven-gloved hand to show us all where to look.

There was a piano in one of the open doorways of the old people's drop-in centre. A lady in a flame-red dress was sitting at it. She started playing and Benny's jaw *dropped*, like mine drops when he plays violin, because he is the one at grade six. The lady's hair was flame-red too, and her shoulders were moving to the rhythm and her hands were roaring up and down the keys like even more flames. She was a lady on fire, and she was captivating.

'Wow,' said Phoebe Dark under her breath. 'Just wow.'

Next to her, unexpectedly and even more

captivating, a man was dancing. He threw himself around to the music and he was graceful and dramatic and extremely willowy and tall. And it was exactly when the man pirouetted on the ball of one foot and turned to face us that Benny put his hand over his own mouth and Phoebe whipped off her sunglasses and we all saw that it was Mr Suarez.

He waved at us and we moved forward like we were being pulled towards him by the tide.

'What are *you* doing here?' we all said, at the same time, us three and Mr Suarez included.

'I live here.' Benny pointed to the eleventh floor.

'My dad works here.' I pointed at my dad.

'I'm with them.' Phoebe Dark pointed at us. 'I'm doing a thing later. About a telescope.'

'I'm visiting my great-aunt Estelita.' Mr

Suarez pointed at the flame-haired lady who was still pounding away on the piano.

The toddlers from the nursery were drifting closer. Some of them were bobbing up and down to the beat and a girl in a princess dress was twirling and twirling. One of the teachers came across to say hello.

'They love it when Estelita plays,' she said.

Grandad and Hedda Wolfe arrived and started setting up their plant stall to sell their trees for bees. They already seemed to know Mr Suarez's great-aunt.

'*Estelita*,' Hedda called in a singsong voice, and Estelita looked up from the keys and smiled her beaming Suarez searchlight smile, but she didn't stop playing. The whole courtyard was dancing. Even Dad's knees were bending and straightening, which is about the closest he gets. Grandad and Miss Wolfe were doing some kind of foxtrot, Claude and Sam were dancing with the toddlers and Angela and Ed were spinning together behind the cold drinks.

Mr Suarez glided over with us to Dad's barbecue.

'Your great-aunt is an incredible musician,' Benny said.

'Do you know,' Mr Suarez said. 'Sometimes my darling Estelita can't remember who I am or even her own name, and sometimes she thinks she is eight or eleven or still in Caracas, but she never, *ever* forgets how to play.'

Just then, Benny's eyes went wide and round like the fullest moon and he pointed towards the furthest corner of the known courtyard. And, as if we hadn't had quite enough surprise and excitement for one day, there was Mrs Hunter, coming towards us slowly with her walking stick, and carrying an enormous slice of Dad's carrot cake on a plate.

'OH!' said Mr Suarez, clapping his hands together, and we watched in dumbstruck SILENCE as he went to help her. The two of them stood together, and he took her arm and Mrs Hunter leaned a little bit against him for support. Chalk and cheese. Glitter and brick dust. In perfect harmony.

'Who's that?' Phoebe said.

'Our old teacher,' Benny said, and I suddenly wondered if, now she was getting better, Mrs Hunter might soon be coming back.

We edged towards them. Because we had already learned her language, even before we knew we were learning it, we did it quietly and slowly, and we waited for her to look up and notice us before we even thought about opening our mouths to speak.

Our old and new teachers were deep in conversation.

Mr Suarez was showing Mrs Hunter picture after picture on his phone. Of our school work and our project and our self-portraits and our very own planets. He was showing her everything, and she didn't rush it. She studied them all in detail.

She said, 'It was about time those tired old kings and queens came down,' and Mr Suarez said, 'And YOU were right. 6C are a *wonderful* crowd.'

She said, 'How is Bailey doing with his numeracy?' and 'Has Clark Watson's mother recovered?' and 'What about . . . ?'

'Oh my goodness,' Benny said. 'She does miss us. She actually does.'

Benny will never get over the fact that Mrs Hunter actually hugged us. For years to come, I already know that we will be doing something, like digging or running or splashing or drawing or even just strolling along, and he will suddenly put his hands on his head and say, 'She did, didn't she? She really did?' and I will tell him, 'Yes, she actually did.'

She was very happy to see us. I am not sure I have found anything so surprising in my entire surprise-filled life.

She said, 'I have been in regular contact with Mr Suarez so I know how hard you are all working.' Then she said, 'And you must be Phoebe Dark, astronomer and first woman on the moon. It is an honour to meet you.' And she shook Phoebe's astonished hand.

'Are you coming back soon?' Benny asked, and Mrs Hunter smiled at him.

'I'm thinking about it,' she said. 'My knee is getting better.'

I looked at Mr Suarez. He had his arm out, supporting her. He was such a bright, warm patch of colour. I was going to miss him when he left. It would be terribly difficult to see him go.

Mrs Hunter was smiling at me now. She said, 'I'm not sure any of us can do without Mr S here.'

'No,' I said.

'So we might work together and share you for a term. You can have two part-time teachers instead of one.'

Benny was grinning. I was doing my absolute best to stay still and not fidget and keep from saying the wrong thing.

'Miss Stilwell thinks it's a good idea,' Mrs Hunter said, and even though she already knew the answer, she added, 'What about you?'

Time off and a new knee has been VERY good for our old teacher, just like school and Plane Tree Gardens and the Hoopers have been VERY good for me.

New things sometimes happen because of something old.

Like how Mrs Hunter made room for Mr Suarez. Or how we wouldn't be here at Grandad's house if it wasn't for Mum and Dad. Or the fact that a star that might look brand-new to us has been blazing for so many millions of years, and its light has taken so long to get to us that the star itself isn't even there any more, even though we can still see it.

Mum says that new things might seem unspoiled and sparkling and shiny, but old things can sparkle too if you take good care of them. Hedda Wolfe said that one person's old was another one's new, like Mum's new dress, which has belonged to at least one other person, or Claude's smile which Dad says was there all along, and just hiding. Or Grandad's telescope, or actually Grandad, come to think of it, who is old to us but new to Hedda, who thinks he is the best thing since sliced bread. Or the first time I saw Jupiter, which was one hundred per cent new to me six days ago, but has been dignifying the night sky and been a part of our solar system for more than four billion years.

And new and old things can exist in a perfect symphony, like Benny and Bach, or the nursery and the seniors' drop-in, or Mrs Hunter's bionic knee, or Mr Suarez's great-aunt Estelita on the piano and the toddlers all dancing. Or Mr Suarez and Mrs Hunter, and Claude and Hedda, who might actually be the real romance of the century, or Phoebe Dark mapping out the stars with her 1976 Skybolt when the rest of us are asleep.

17

It has suddenly struck me, like a bolt of lightning, that this time, for the first time ever, I don't think I want to move. I have had enough of seeing packing boxes and hearing whispers and listening to Grandad hinting about new horizons when Claude says that there isn't even room to swing a cat. I want to stay. Right here. Where we all are. In one place at 48 Plane Tree Gardens.

When I say this at the dinner table, Mum says, 'Move where?'

Grandad says, 'Why would you want to do that?' and Claude says, 'What's this?' and, 'It's the first I've heard of it.'

Dad says, 'Why on *earth* would we move now when we are all only just getting settled?'

'Oh, good,' I say, breathing out and tucking into my cheese-free lasagne. We are all vegans now because of Claude's campaigning. At least three times a week. 'I must have been overhearing wrongly.'

'Overhearing has a habit of doing that,' says Mum, but she winks at me to show she isn't the least bit cross.

Mum and Dad are very happy with their new sofa bed. And Claude says she doesn't really mind sharing a room with me, given that we are lucky to have one. She has recently added homelessness to the list of things that deserve caring about. She and Sam are volunteering at the food bank on Saturdays and she has already persuaded Grandad to donate his spare produce, and most of the tins that have been hiding in the back of his larder 'since 1994'.

Grandad has also donated his Skybolt to Phoebe Dark. She keeps it locked in a cupboard at school, because her brothers can't touch it there, and she is hoping to start astronomy club on a Friday. Miss Stilwell is on the hunt for a responsible grown-up to supervise.

So we are staying for now. This is a big relief. But my family does have one surprise for me.

The blackbird's-egg shed has been tidied, but not just so that Grandad can keep his seed packets in it, filed like my friends' addresses, from A to Z.

'It's for you,' Hedda says. 'A little quiet space.'

'For *me*?' I say, and everyone nods and follows me out into the garden.

Buster is sitting by the open door. He is as still as a statue, until he spots a butterfly and bounds off like a cheetah after a gazelle.

Inside the shed, there is a desk and a lamp, spilling light out into the evening, and a blanket, for if it gets a bit chilly. There are two chairs and a stool, just in case I want to have a friend or two round.

It is the best, most unexpected, out-of-the-blue present I have ever had.

On my desk there is a note from Benny that says: 'SURPRISE! See you tomorrow. I will bring snacks.'

And Phoebe Dark has dropped off a present, wrapped in brown paper. She has written my address on the front, even though she must have delivered it by hand, secretly, when I wasn't looking.

It says:

JOY APPLEBLOOM,
48 Plane Tree Gardens,
England, Europe,
The Earth, The Solar System,
Orion Arm, The Milky Way,
The Local Group, The Virgo Supercluster,
The Known Universe

This is a much better place to live than the square root of nowhere. And inside the parcel is a hand-painted sign for my new, very own

shed. Black, with silver writing, and twinkling
with stars.

It says, in perfect star-spangled, silvery
writing –

Acknowledgements

THANK YOUS to Veronique Baxter for everything. To Rachel Denwood and Lowri Ribbons for all things words. To Claire Lefevre for the joyful illustrations and Emily Hearn for her work on design.

To boephedork for letting me use your name, to Robin for Trees for Bees and to Sophie Hartman and Di Blunt for your constant reading and brilliant minds.

And to Livi Sanna Raatgever. Writer. Climate Striker. The all-round original seed on the breeze.

For more information on real-life tree planting, please visit www.ecologi.com.

Look out
for more
JOY

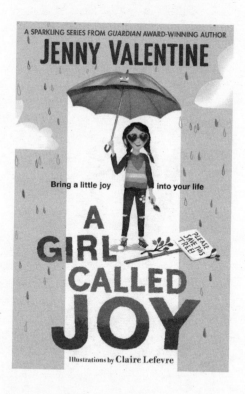

Turn the page for a sneak peek!

1

There is absolutely no storybook magic in our family. We don't have a grandad who can fly, or an uncle who is busy somewhere building a time machine, or parents who are world-famous wizards-in-hiding. Our grandad walks with a stick, we have zero uncles, and our mum and dad have out-of-the-blue started saying things like, 'Put that back where it came from,' and, 'Where's your school uniform?' and,

'Please hoover your room immediately.'

According to my big sister, Claude, this makes us extremely ordinary. But we have never been ordinary. And I don't think we should be ready to start now.

I'm not pretending there haven't been some big changes. Things are feeling very pedestrian around here, that's for sure. Extremely squidged in. And it goes without saying that nobody has a wand to get us out of trouble, or their own super-helpful pack of wolves, or a lump of rock that can speak in whole sentences. There are no parallel universes under our sinks, or other worlds in our wardrobes, or perfect tiny humans between our walls. There are cleaning products, and clothes, and possibly mice. I don't have shoes that rush about all over the place with a mind of their own. I have one pair of trainers that are at least one size too small, and I am not ready to throw them away yet because they have been with me everywhere, on so many adventures. The washing machine won't get the grass stains out of Claude's precious new jeans, and right now, Dad can't get rid of the coffee he spilled on Grandad's carpet. So I am pretty sure that none of us can make stuff disappear.

But the thing is, there is more than one kind of magic. It shouldn't have to mean the same as impossible, and only be allowed to happen in stories. That just doesn't seem right to me. Claude says our definitions of magic are different, and that I am always marvelling at something or other for no good reason because I am way too easily impressed. I am twenty-four seven on the lookout for some everyday, actually real-life magic because that's the kind I believe in, and, to be honest, I think we could do with some.

When I say so, Claude does one of her semi-professional eye-rolls and says, 'Oh, yeah? Well. Good luck with that.'

When you don't have storybook magic, your problems are less fancy and not as much fun to fix. For example, Dad has stuck a big heavy book about trees over the coffee stain, in a hurry, and now it is lurking there in the middle of the room where it doesn't belong, like a suitcase in a canal. Any minute, somebody, most likely Grandad, is going to bump into it and find out the truth. Claude says it's not going to be pretty when he does, and it is only a matter of time. Even with my talent for positive thinking, I am starting to think she might have got that one right.

I am ten, and Claude is thirteen.

She smells like cherries and wears black make-up all over her eyes. She has the straightest, whitest teeth and the shiniest toothpaste smile I have ever seen. When she is happy, she looks like an advert for the dentist, but at the moment that isn't very often. Dad says Claude's toothpaste smile has become a bit like a meteor shower, because it might only happen once or twice a year, and if you blink you'll miss it.

We saw a meteor shower in California, when I was six and Claude was nine. The sky rained stars for hours and hours, and I fell asleep before it was finished. You would have to do a long old blink to miss that.

Claude is short for Claudia Eloise, and

rhymes with bored, which these days is just about right. Ever since we got back to the UK and moved into Grandad's house, she is always complaining that nothing is worth doing and there is less than nothing to do. Mum and Dad have started calling her the brick wall, but not so she can hear them. They whisper it behind their hands, but I'm not sure they need to bother. As far as I can tell, she has pretty much completely stopped listening to anything they have to say.

Mum and Dad's names are Rina and Dan, short for Marina Jane Blake and Daniel Samson Applebloom. They have been hyper-distracted and crazy-busy since we arrived, doing out-of-character and mind-bendingly ordinary things like applying for jobs that involve zero travel, signing up at the doctor's, and shoe-horning us into schools. These are not activities we are used to our parents being busy at. In fact, they are the total opposite of what we have spent our whole lives being taught to expect. It is very unsettling. Claude reckons Mum and Dad had radical personality transplants, like, overnight, when we weren't looking. She says they might not actually be our original parents any more, and we need to stay alert, because absolutely anything could be about to happen.

I say, 'Are you sure they're the only ones?' because right now I would bet money on the fact she's had the personality transplant too. She definitely isn't acting like my original sister. She isn't nearly as much fun as she used to be.

I haven't had anything transplanted. I am exactly the same as ever, even though everything else has changed. My name can't be shortened and I don't have a middle one. It is what it is, and everyone just calls me Joy.

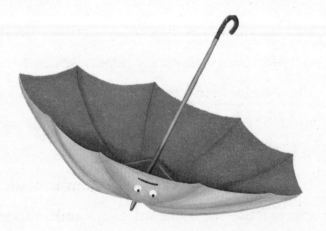

2

The here that we have got to is Grandad's house.

His name is Thomas Blake, and he is Mum's dad, although sometimes I find it hard to believe they are even related. I would never ever pick them out of a line-up of fathers and daughters, unless I knew. Not in a million. Grandad is sort of faint and blurry, like someone drew him with a soft pencil, and Mum is marker-pen dark. Mum is loud and bombastic and colourful, and Grandad is more narrow and faded and quiet. Mum is a socialist, which is a long political word for being good-at-sharing, and Grandad? Well, Grandad is not. Mum says we are world citizens and should support the free movement of people across the globe, and I think Grandad would prefer to put a nice tall fence around this one little island, and cover it in great big signs that say,

NO TRESPASSING
and
PRIVATE PROPERTY
and
KEEP OUT.

Our family does not see eye to eye with Grandad on a long list of things. I think that's why we spend so much time talking to him about the weather.

The letters on his doormat say Mr T. E. Blake but he won't tell me what the E is for, so I have decided to guess. I have been allowing myself a new guess every day. I don't think I am close to getting it right, but so far he has not decided to correct me, so I'm just going to carry on trying.

Thomas Elephant Blake's face is full of pockets and pouches like a backpack and when he speaks, the pockets and pouches fill and empty with air. The letters he gets are mostly catalogues for slippers that plug into the wall, and baths with actual doors in the side for getting in and out, and hearing aids disguised as reading glasses. I think the catalogues are brilliant and inventive, but Thomas Eggcup Blake does not agree. He says that having permanently cold feet and not being able to climb in and out of the bath or hear and see properly are not reasons to celebrate. I think he says that about a lot of things. I'm not sure he is really the celebrating kind. He is mostly grey from head to toe, like he has just walked through a room where the ceiling fell in. Claude says that wouldn't happen at Thomas Eagle-Eye Blake's house, where everything looks scared of being out of place. She says the ceilings wouldn't be brave enough. They actually wouldn't dare.

Mum is keen for us all to get along like a house on fire, another thing my sister says would never happen, seeing as Grandad goes around at night switching every single plug socket off. We aren't supposed to make up our minds about him yet, because we don't know him well enough to reach a proper verdict. Mum says, Family is Family is Family, whatever side of the fence you're on, whatever your domestic habits or whatever you believe. Dad says we all need to be patient with each other, and spend more time together, and let the dust settle.

Claude says, 'Fat chance,' and I think, 'What dust? There isn't even one speck,' but they both say that it will be worth the wait, and that eventually the real Grandad will emerge like a butterfly coming out of its chrysalis, or at least a snake shedding its old skin.

I have seen thousands and thousands of Monarch butterflies hatching in Mexico, turning the hillsides a living, quivering red, and I have watched a rattlesnake leave behind its own skin outside in the hot sand, quick and papery as a crayon wrapper. So I wonder exactly how soon and how spectacular Thomas Extravaganza Blake's big reveal might actually be.

Claude shakes her head at me, and then at Mum and Dad, and then at our new squashed-in world in general, and says something muffled and full of gravel about nobody bothering to hold their breath.

Bring a little

JOY

into your life with
more books from

JENNY VALENTINE

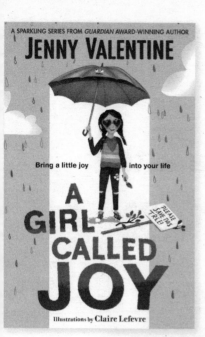

A SPARKLING SERIES FROM *GUARDIAN* AWARD-WINNING AUTHOR

JENNY VALENTINE

Bring a little joy   into your life

A GIRL CALLED JOY

Illustrations by Claire Lefevre

A SPARKLING SERIES FROM *GUARDIAN* AWARD-WINNING AUTHOR

JENNY VALENTINE

BE KIND

Send a little JOY into the world

LOVE FROM JOY

Illustrations by Claire Lefevre

A SPARKLING SERIES FROM *GUARDIAN* AWARD-WINNING AUTHOR

JENNY VALENTINE

PLANET JOY

Find your place. Find your JOY.

Illustrations by Claire Lefevre